"He is waking! Someone get His Grace and Her Ladyship immediately."

He opened his eyes at last and tried to sit up, but the room was still a blur, and his back did not want to support him.

Who the devil was *Her Ladyship?*

Something smelled wonderful. No. It was someone. Roses and cinnamon, close at his side. Muslin leaning against his bare arm, and warm silky skin touching his shoulder, then smoothing the hair on his brow. His senses were returning to him in a series of pleasant surprises.

He saw a perfect, heart-shaped face.

"Is someone going to explain to me what has happened, or will you leave me to guess? Did I take ill in the night?"

"We heard nothing from you for months. When Justine brought you home, you were in no state to say anything. There had been an accident."

"Who is this Justine?"

"It seems there is much you have lost, and much that must be explained to you. But first and foremost, you must know this—the woman before you now is Lady Felkirk." He paused again. "William, may I introduce to you your wife, Justine."

* * *

The Truth About Lady Felkirk
Harlequin® Historical #1205—October 2014

Author Note

My first career, long before I settled into life as a writer, was theatrical costuming. During the theater season, I spent eight hours a day, six days a week sewing for others. In my spare time, I sewed for myself. Over the years I have tried the majority of fiber arts. I taught myself to knit in high school. It took two or three tries to learn tatting. It took fifty years, and the advent of the internet instructional videos, for me to learn to crochet.

The one thing I've never tried, and never will, is bobbin lace. I have watched it being done and I know I am far too impatient to manage even a simple project. And considering the mess my newest cat has made of the knitting basket, I can only imagine what he would do if given a pillow trailing a lot of threads, with bobbins just waiting to be batted.

How fortunate that I have Justine to work through any of my subconscious, lace-making urges.

Happy reading.

Christine Merrill

The Truth About Lady Felkirk

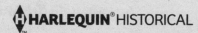
HARLEQUIN® HISTORICAL

Recycling programs
for this product may
not exist in your area.

ISBN-13: 978-0-373-29805-1

THE TRUTH ABOUT LADY FELKIRK

Copyright © 2014 by Christine Merrill

Printed in U.S.A.

www.Harlequin.com

Available from Harlequin® Historical and
CHRISTINE MERRILL

And in Harlequin Historical *Undone!* ebooks

*part of the Silk & Scandal series
ΔLadies in Disgrace
**The Sinner and the Saint

**Did you know that these novels are also
available as ebooks? Visit www.Harlequin.com.**

To Jim: after thirty years,
you must be near to sainthood.

CHRISTINE MERRILL

lives on a farm in Wisconsin, U.S.A., with her husband, two sons and too many pets—all of whom
would like her to get off the computer so they can
check their email. She has worked by turns in theater costuming, where she was paid to play with period ballgowns, and as a librarian, where she spent
the day surrounded by books. Writing historical romance combines her love of good stories and fancy
dress with her ability to stare out the window and
make stuff up.

Chapter One

Everything hurt.

William Felkirk did not bother to open his eyes, but lay still and examined the thought. It was an exaggeration. Everything ached. Only his head truly hurt. A slow, thumping throb came from the back of it, punctuating each new idea.

He swallowed with effort. There was no saliva to soothe the process. How much had he been drinking, to get to this state? He could not seem to remember. The party at Adam's house, which had been a celebration of his nephew's christening, was far too sedate for him to have ended like this. But he could not recall having gone anywhere after. And since he was in Wales, where would he have gone?

His eyelids were still too heavy to open, but he did not need vision to find the crystal carafe by the bedside. A drink of water would help. His arm flailed bonelessly, numb fingers unable to close on the glass.

There was a gasp on the other side of the room and the shatter of porcelain as an ornament was dropped and broken. Clumsy maids. The girl had been cleaning around him, as though he was a piece of furniture. Was it really necessary to shout 'He is waking!' so that anyone in the hall could hear?

Then there were hurried footsteps to the door and a voice called for someone to get his Grace and her ladyship immediately.

He opened his eyes at last and tried to sit up, but the room was still a blur and his back did not want to support him. He stared at the ceiling and what little he could see of the bedposts. It was still his brother's house. But Penelope had never been a ladyship, even before marrying Adam. Even now, she laughed about not feeling graceful enough to be her Grace, the Duchess of Bellston. Though she was just out of childbed, she was not so frail as to cede her duties as hostess to another. Who the devil was *her ladyship*?

He must have misheard. But the rueful shake of his head made the pain worse, as did the thundering of steps on the stairs and in the hall. Could not a man bear the shame of a hangover in privacy? He tried to sit up again, and as he did, he felt an arm at his back and hands lifting him, like a child, to settle him against the pillows.

'There's a good fellow.' Adam was treating him like an invalid. It must be even worse than he thought. 'A drink of water, perhaps?' But instead of the cup he expected, there was a damp rag pressed to his lips.

Will spat and turned his head away. '…Hell?' He must be parched for he could not seem to speak properly. But it had been enough to make his displeasure known.

'You want a glass?' Adam seemed to find this extraordinary. 'Where is Justine? Find her, quickly.'

The rim of the cup met his lips. He reached for it, felt his arm flop, then tremble, and then the hand of his older brother was there to steady it so he could drink.

Crystal goblet. Crystal water. Cool and sweet, trickling, then coursing down his throat, which still felt as though it was full of cobwebs. Some of the pounding in his skull subsided. He paused. 'Better.' His voice croaked, but it was clearer.

There was another feminine gasp from the doorway.

'He is waking,' Adam said, softly, urgently. 'Come to his side.'

'I dare not.' It was a woman's voice: a melodious alto, with the faintest hint of an accent to it.

'After so long, you must be the first thing he sees.' He could feel Adam rise, and, as he watched, another hand came to guide the water glass.

Something smelled wonderful. No. It was someone. Roses, and cinnamon, close at his side. Muslin leaning against his bare arm and warm silky skin touching his shoulder, then smoothing the hair on

his brow. His senses were returning to him, in a series of pleasant surprises.

When his vision could focus past the fingers on
the cup, he saw a perfect, heart-shaped face, looking
worriedly into his. It was the sort of face that made
him wish he could paint, or at least draw, so that he
might carry a copy of it with him for ever. Her eyes
were the strange green gold of coins at the bottom
of a fountain and he could not seem to stop staring
at them. They were sad eyes and fearful. For a moment, he thought he saw the beginnings of a tear in
one. Her pink lips trembled. Her hair was a mix of
sunset golds and reds, partially obscured under a
plain muslin cap. The curls swayed gently, as though
their owner was eased away from him.

'Do not be afraid,' he said. Why was she here?
And why was she so hesitant? He was not sure of
much, least of all who this might be. But he was quite
sure he did not want her to be in fear of him. Adam
had been right. To wake to this was a gift, especially
when one had such a damnable headache.

'After all that has happened, he is concerned for
you?' Adam gave a short, satisfied laugh. 'You have
not changed at all, then, Will. We had so feared...'
His brother's voice cracked with emotion.

'Is it true?' Adam's wife, Penny, was here now,
somewhere by the door. She was out of breath, as if
she had rushed to the room.

Adam hissed at her to be silent.

'The more, the merrier,' Will muttered, still without the energy to turn away yet another visitor to his bedside. But when he turned his face to the duchess, something was wrong. Very wrong, in fact. She appeared to be pregnant. That could not be right. Just yesterday, he'd thought her rather thin. He'd enquired after her health and had listened to his brother's complaints that the recent birth had taken too much from her. Today, she stood in the doorway of his bedroom, plump and healthy.

Will frowned. If it was a joke, it was both elaborate and pointless. The whole family was watching him, as though waiting for something. He had no idea what they expected. His head was swimming again. He went to rub his temple, but it took all his strength to lift his own arm.

The woman at his side grasped the hand and brought it down again, rubbing some feeling back into the fingers, flexing joints and massaging muscles. Then she laid it carefully on the counterpane and brought her own fingers up to stroke his forehead. Damn, but it felt good. If he were not still so tired, he'd have sent the family away, to test the extent of her familiarity with his body. Though she had hesitated at first, she did not seem the least bit shy now.

He relaxed back into the pillows that had been leaned against the headboard and sighed. Then, slowly, carefully, he flexed the fingers of each hand. It was difficult, as was moving his toes. But when next he raised his hand, he was able to gesture for the water without embarrassing himself. His beautiful nurse brought the glass to his lips again.

He licked a drop off his dry lips and swallowed again. 'Is someone going to explain to me what has happened, or will you leave me to guess? Did I take ill in the night?'

'Explain?' Adam, again, speaking for the group. 'What do you remember of the last months, Will?'

'The Season, of course,' he answered, wishing he could give a dismissive wave. 'That blonde chit you were forcing on me. Why you think you can choose my wife, when I had no say in yours, I have no idea. And coming up to Wales with you for the christening. What did you put in the punch to get me into such a state? Straight gin?'

He meant to joke. But the faces around him were shocked to silence. Adam cleared his throat. 'The christening was six months ago.'

'Certainly not.' He could remember it, as clearly as he could remember anything. It seemed distant, of course. But he had just woken up. When his head cleared…

'Six months,' Adam repeated. 'After the party you left and would not tell us where you were going. You said you would be returning with a surprise.'

'And what was it?' Will asked. If he was here now, he must have returned, with a story that would explain his current condition.

'We heard nothing from you, for months. When Justine brought you home, you were in no state to say anything. There had been an accident. She thought it best that you be with your family, when…' Adam's voice broke again and he looked away.

'Who is this Justine?' Will said, looking around. But judging by the shocked expression on the face of the woman holding his hand, the question answered itself.

'You really don't remember?' she said. And he did not. Although how he could have forgotten a face or a voice like that, he was not sure.

'I remember the christening,' he repeated. 'But I have no recollection of you at all.'

The gold eyes in front of him were open wide now, incredulous.

Adam cleared his throat again, the little noise he tended to make when he was about to be diplomatic. 'It seems there is much you have lost and much that must be explained to you. But first and foremost, you must know this. The woman before you now is Lady Felkirk.' He paused again. 'William, may I introduce to you your wife, Justine.'

'I have no wife.' He'd had more than enough of this foolishness and swung his feet out of the bed to stand and walk away.

Or at least he tried. Instead, he flopped on the mattress like a beached fish, spilling the water and sliding halfway out of bed before his brother could steady him, and muscle him back to the centre.

'It is all right. As long as you are getting better, it does not matter.' There was the voice of the ministering angel again, his supposed wife. What had they called her? Justine?

The name, though it was as beautiful as its owner, held no resonance.

Adam leaned over the bed again, smiling, although the grin was somewhat stained. 'Justine brought you home some two months ago, and you have lain insensible since then. I feared you would never...' There was another pause, followed by a deep sigh. Perhaps fatherhood had made Adam soft, for Will could not recall ever hearing him sound near to tears. 'The doctors did not give us much hope. To find you awake and almost yourself again...'

So he'd cracked his skull. He did not remember it, but it certainly explained the throbbing in his head. 'What happened?'

'A fall from a horse.'

That seemed possible. He sometimes overreached himself, when in the saddle. But his old friend, Jupiter, was the most steady of beasts, as long as he held the reins. And a wife... He stared pointedly at the woman leaning over him, waiting for her to add some explanation.

'We were on our honeymoon,' the woman said, gently, as though trying to prod the memory from him. 'We met in Bath, at the beginning of summer.'

Still, nothing. What had he been doing in Bath? He abhorred the place, with its foul-tasting water and the meddling mamas of girls who could not make a proper match in London.

'I am sure marriage must have been in your plans when you left us,' Penny said, encouraging him. 'You did promise us a surprise. But really, we had no idea how welcome it would be. When Justine returned with you…' She gave an emotional pause again, just as his brother had done. 'She has been so good to you. To all of us, really. She never lost hope.' Under the guise of wiping her fogged spectacles, Penny withdrew a handkerchief and dabbed at her eyes.

Only the woman, Justine, seemed to take it all calmly, as though a husband returning from death's door with no memory of her was a thing that happened to everyone. When she spoke, her voice was unbroken and matter-of-fact. 'You will be all right now. Everything is better than we could have hoped.'

'As if being concussed and losing half a year of one's life is a thing to be celebrated.' He glared at her. Perhaps this lovely stranger had done nothing to deserve his anger. Or perhaps she had got him drunk and knocked him on the head so she could pretend to be his wife.

But that made no sense. He lacked the money and title necessary to be the target of such intriguing. If she meant him ill, why did she bring him home, afterwards? Why bother to nurse him back to health?

The mysterious Justine ignored his dark look and smiled down at him. 'It is to be celebrated. The physician said you would never wake, yet, you did. Now that you can eat properly, you will grow stronger.' But did he see a fleeting shadow in her eyes, as though his recovery was something less than a blessing?

Perhaps she was as confused as he, after all. Or perhaps he had hurt her. He had taken the trouble to marry her, only to forget her entirely. Now, he was snapping at her, blaming her for his sore head. Had he treated her thus, before the accident? Perhaps the marriage had been a mistake. If so, he could hardly blame her for a passing desire that his prolonged illness would end with her freedom.

When he looked again, her face was as cloudless as a summer day. The doubt had been an illusion, caused by his own paranoia. When he was stronger and had a chance to question her, things would be clearer. For now, he must rein in his wild thoughts and wait. He shook his head and immediately regretted it, as the pain, which had been ebbing, came rushing back.

She leaned closer, reaching across him for a cool cloth that lay beside the bed, pressing it against his forehead.

How did she know it would soothe him? It did not matter. If she guessed, she guessed correctly. He took her hand and squeezed it in what he hoped she would know as gratitude. But though the pain was lessening, his doubts were not. There was nothing the least bit familiar about the shape of the hand he held. Surely, if he had married her, the joining should not feel so entirely alien. As soon as he could do so without appearing awkward, he withdrew his hand.

She made sure the compress was secure and withdrew her own hands, folding them neatly in her lap as though equally relieved to be free of him.

While the two of them were clearly uncomfortable with each other, the rest of the room was ecstatic. 'Whenever you are ready, we will bring you downstairs,' Penny said. 'Perhaps we can procure a Bath chair so that you might take sun in the garden.'

'Nonsense.' The compress slipped as he tried to struggle to his feet again. This time he made slightly more progress. He was able to swing both legs over the edge of the bed and sit up. Almost immediately, the dizziness took him and he felt himself sliding to the side.

Once again, Adam rushed in, taking his arm and holding him upright. 'Easy. Do not try too much at once. There will be no Bath chair, if you do not wish it. You may go at your own pace. I am sure you will be walking well on your own in no time at all.'

'But you do not need to do it now,' Penny insisted. 'Rest is still important. And quiet. For now, we will leave the two of you alone.'

'No.'

'Yes.' He and the woman spoke simultaneously.

'You need your rest,' Justine said, laying a hand gently on his chest to try to ease him back down to the mattress. 'There will be time later for us to speak.'

'I have had more than enough rest,' he said. 'If you are all to be believed, I have been asleep for months.'

She was probably right. His head ached from even this small bit of activity. He needed time to think. But before that, he needed answers. Despite the innocent look on the beautiful face in front of him, Justine knew more than she had said.

'Leave, all of you. Please,' he added after noticing the shocked looks on their faces at his short temper. 'But send for my valet. After all this time in bed, I want to wash and dress. Until he arrives, I will talk to my wife.'

'Of course,' his brother said, with a relieved smile. 'If you are well enough, you can come down to dinner, or we will have a tray sent up. Either way,' he stepped forward again and clasped Will's hand in a firm grip, 'it is good to see you recovering. Come, Penny, I am sure they have much to discuss that does not concern us.'

Once they were gone and the door shut behind him, he was alone in a room with a woman who claimed to be his wife. He suppressed a rush of panic. He was still too weak to defend himself, should she not be as kind as she appeared. But why could he imagine such a sweet-faced thing as a danger to him? If she'd meant him harm, she'd have had ample opportunity before now.

Still, should not a new bride be happier to see her husband recovering? If she loved him, why was she standing at the side of his bed, mute like a criminal in the dock? There was something wrong about her. It was one of many things he could not place.

She seemed to realise this as well, for she attempted a hesitant smile and slipped easily back into the role of caregiver. 'Is there something I can get for you? Anything that might give you comfort?'

'What a good little nurse you are, to be so solicitous.' he said, not feeling particularly grateful for it. 'At the moment, there is nothing I need, other than an end to this charade.'

'There is no charade,' she said, looking more puzzled than frightened. 'We are not trying to trick you. You were injured and have been unconscious for several months. Come to the window and you shall see. The christening was at Easter time. It is no longer spring, or even summer. The leaves are falling and the night air is chill.'

'I do not need for you to tell me the weather,' he grumbled, glancing at the grey sky beyond the glass. 'I can see that for myself. And I know I was injured, for I still feel the pain of it.' He ran a careful hand through his hair, surprised at the crease in the scalp. 'But that does not explain the rest.'

'What else is there?' she said, though she must know full well what he meant.

'It does not explain you. Who are you, really? And who are you to me?' He looked full into the wide green eyes. 'For I would swear before God that you are not my wife.'

'William,' she said, in a convincingly injured tone.

'That is my name. And what is yours?'

'Justine, of course.'

'And before you married me?' he said, unable to help sneering at such an unlikely prospect.

'My surname? It was de Bryun.' She paused as though waiting for the bit of information to jar loose some memory. But nothing came.

'So you say,' he replied. 'I suppose next you will tell me you are an orphan.'

'Yes,' she said, unable to keep the hurt from her voice.

In a day, he might regret being so cavalier about her misery. At the moment, he had problems of his own. 'So you have no one to verify your identity.'

'I have a sister,' she added. 'But she was not present at the time of our wedding, nor was your family.'

'I married without my family's knowledge?' Penny had hinted at as much. But it still made no sense. 'So neither of us considered the feelings of others in this. We just suddenly...' with effort, he managed to snap his fingers '...decided to wed.'

'We discussed it beforehand,' she assured him. 'You said there would be time after. You said your brother had done something much the same to you.'

As he had. That marriage had been as sudden as this one. And Adam had admitted that he could not remember his wedding either. But while circumstances were similar, he had more sense than Adam and would never have behaved in that way. 'You could have learned the details of Adam's wedding anywhere,' he said.

She sighed, as though she were in a classroom,

being forced to recite. 'But I did not learn it anywhere. I learned it from you. You told me that your
father's name was John, your mother's name was
Mary. They were Duke and Duchess of Bellston, of
course. You had one sister, who died at birth. And
you told me all about your brother. It was why I
brought you here. Why would I have done that, if
not for love of you?'

This was a puzzle. He rubbed his temple, for
though he was sure there was a logical explanation
for it, searching for it made his head ache. 'You could
have got any of that from a peerage book.'

'Or you could have told me,' she said, patiently.
'And it is not so unusual that I have no parents. You
have none either.'

That was perfectly true. So why did it seem somehow significant that she had none? He shook his
head, half-expecting it to rattle as he did so, for he
still felt like a broken china doll. 'I suspect I can quiz
you for hours and you will have an answer for everything. But there is one question I doubt you will
answer to my satisfaction. What would have moti-
vated me to take a wife?'

'You said you loved me.' Her lip trembled, though
she did not look near tears. 'And I did not wish to lie
with you, until we were married.'

It was not a flattering explanation. But it made
more sense than anything else she had said. 'I can
believe that I might have wanted to lie with you. My
eyesight is fine, though my memory is not.' He stared

up at the magnificent hair, still mostly obscured by her very sensible cap. Tired and confused as he was, he still wanted to snatch the muslin away, so that he might see it in all its glory. 'You are a beauty. And you know it, do you not? You are not going to pretend that you are unaware of the effect you have on men. Why did you choose me?'

'Because I thought you were kind and would be a good husband to me,' she said. There was something in her voice that implied she had been disappointed to find otherwise. Then she cast down her eyes. 'And you are right. I cannot help the way I look, or the reaction of others.'

'I do not see why you would wish to,' he answered honestly. But when he looked closely, her face held a mixture of regret and defiance, as though she very much wished she were plain and not pretty. Her clothing was almost too modest, nearly as plain as a servant's. The cap she wore was not some vain concoction of lace and ribbons, but undecorated linen. If she was attempting to disguise her assets, she had failed. The simple setting made the jewel of her beauty glow all the more brightly.

'You are acting as if, now that you have what you want, it is somehow my fault that the results do not please you.' She absently straightened the cap on her head, hiding a few more of the escaping curls. 'I did not seduce you into a marriage you did not wish. Nor did I injure you and leave you to your fate. I doubt I can prove to your satisfaction that things are just as I claim. But can you prove that I have done anything, other than to give you what you wanted from me, and care for you when it resulted in misfortune? You are alive today because of my treatment of you. I am sorry that I cannot offer more than that.'

To this, he had no answer. If she truly was his wife, she was a very patient woman. She had reason to snap at his harsh treatment of her. But there was no real anger in her voice, only a tired resignation as she accepted his doubt. If it weren't for the troublesome void where their past should have resided, he would have believed in an instant and apologiscd.

'I will admit that I owe you my gratitude,' he said. 'But for the moment, your help is not needed. Please, go and prepare for dinner. Perhaps I will see you at table. We can speak again later.'

'I will welcome it, my lord.'

She was lying, of course. She rose from the bed and offered an obedient curtsy, before leaving the room. But there was an eagerness in her step that made her simple exit seem almost like an escape.

Chapter Two

He did not remember her.

Justine de Bryun stopped just beyond William Felkirk's door and tried to contain the excitement and relief she felt at this convenient amnesia. She must channel that tangle of emotion into an appropriate response for a woman whose husband had awakened like Lazarus, before someone saw and questioned her. Felkirk had asked more than enough questions during the difficult conversation that had just occurred. She did not need more questioning from the duke and duchess. At least not until she could discover a way out of the mess she had created.

Penny was waiting for her, a little way down the hall, trying to pretend that she was not interested in a description of what had happened, when she and William had been alone together. She must try to come up with something that was not a total lie. Since coming here, she had lied too much to her host-

ess and felt guilty each time. What had Penny ever
done to deserve such treatment? From the first, the
duchess had offered the hand of friendship and the
sympathy of a sister.

While Justine had reason enough to hate the Felkirk family, there was no reason her animosity need
extend to a woman who had married into it. Nor did
it feel right to hate the heir, who was nothing more
than an innocent babe. The duke, who was the true
head of the family, had been kindness himself as well
and earned some measure of forgiveness.

That left only William Felkirk. His meddling in
her affairs had earned him the whole share of any
punishment for the family's past sins. His slow recovery had been more than sufficient to satisfy her
desire for vengeance.

It had been too much, if she was honest. Her father had died a quick death. But William Felkirk
had lingered on the brink for months, wasting away
in endless sleep. On several occasions, she'd been
surprised to find herself praying that God would
be merciful and release him. When the prayers had
gone unanswered, she had given him what Christian
comfort she could.

Or she had until the moment he'd awoken and
begun causing trouble again.

Penny was coming towards her now, hands outstretched, ready to celebrate or console, as was needed.
Justine discovered she did not need to dissemble
much, for her lip actually trembled in what was likely

the beginning of tears. Once again, she was alone and helpless in a situation she had done little to cause and was not able to control. While the Duchess of Bellston did not appear to wish her ill, Justine had seen how quickly supposed friends became enemies when they knew one had nowhere to turn. She must be on her guard. 'He does not know me,' she said, softly, glancing back at the bedroom behind her. 'And he does not believe we are married.'

The duchess enfolded her in a motherly hug. 'There, there. It will be all right, I'm sure. Now that he is recovering, it will only be a matter of time before he recalls what you once were to each other.'

'Of course,' Justine answered, as though that was not another reason for tears. Felkirk's total absence of memory was the best news she'd had in ages. He had forgotten the worst of it and she might still escape punishment. One could not be complicit in an attack on a noble family and avoid the gallows. She had known her fate was sealed the day that she had found him on the salon floor in a pool of blood. Even if she had wished him ill, William Felkirk both recovered and amnesiac was a gift straight from God.

Of course, it also meant he could not recall the things she actually wished to know. And that was most vexing. Without that, why had she bothered to save him?

Penny patted her shoulder. 'As soon as he has recovered his strength, you can return to the old manor.

That is his house now and will be yours as well. We will be less than a mile away if you need us. Familiar surroundings will have the memories flooding back in no time.'

A flood of memory was the last thing she needed. Moving to Felkirk's own home would draw her even deeper into the ruse she had created. They would be alone, with no duke and duchess to help her deflect Lord Felkirk's endless questions. 'It will be quite different, being alone with him there,' she said, trying to keep the resignation from her voice.

'We will be just down the road,' Penny replied cheerfully. 'We can come for visits or for dinner, as soon as you are ready to receive us.'

They would come, and leave again, before bedtime. Justine would be left to manage the nights, alone with a strange man who would expect more than nursing from a beautiful woman who claimed to be his wife. What had he said to her, just now? *You are not going to pretend that you are unaware of the effect you have on men.*

Montague had said something similar, when he had informed her of what her future would be. Now, it would be happening all over again. When he was unconscious, William Felkirk had been as pale and beautiful as a statue. But awake she could see the virile strength that had been dormant. The blood was returning to his lips and the observant blue eyes turned on her already sparkled with interest. Soon there would be another, very male response to her presence in his bedroom. She could not help herself, she shivered.

Without a word, Penny slipped the shawl from her own shoulders and wrapped it around Justine. 'You are tired, of course. You have worked so hard to make him well again. And it has not turned out as you expected.'

'No, it has not,' Justine admitted. She had assumed, no matter what she did to prevent it, he would die. She would enter the sickroom some morning to find the patient stiff and cold. It had made her search all the harder for evidence of her father, or a sign that he had delivered the jewels he'd been carrying, when he'd died. If she could have got her hands on them, she might have disappeared before anyone discovered her lies.

Then, it had occurred to her that, if William Felkirk died, it might be easier just to stay as she was, allowing the duke and duchess to comfort her in her mourning. Montague would not dare tell his half of the truth, for fear that she would tell hers. In a year, when she'd cast off her black, there might be holidays, and summer, and a Season in London with balls and parties…

And where would that leave Margot? As usual, the thought doused all happiness like cold water. How unfair was it that any thought of her beloved little sister should be wrapped in negatives?

As they walked down the hall and towards the main stairs, Penny continued to chatter on, filling the tense silence with descriptions of a happy future that could never be. 'Above all, do not worry yourself over his behaviour today. I am sure he loves you. But the truth was quite a shock to him.' She hesitated, then added, 'The doctors said there might be changes in his character, because of the accident.'

'True,' Justine agreed. How could she tell? She knew nothing of his character, after only one brief meeting. When he had entered the shop, she had thought him handsome and pleasant enough. But his initial smile had faded, when he'd realised who, and what, she was.

Penny sensed her unease and added, 'He will remember you, in time, I am sure. You have nothing to worry about.'

'I am sure you are right.' The words were true, even if the smile that accompanied them was not. He would remember her. She must be long gone before that happened, even if it meant returning to the life with Montague that she had hoped to escape.

They were at the door of her bedroom now and she gave the duchess a light kiss on the cheek to prove that it was, indeed, all right. 'I think I should like to lie down before dinner.'

'Of course,' Penny replied. 'Now that your husband is better, you must take care of yourself. And you will want to look your best for him, should Will be able to come to down for his meal.'

Justine smiled and nodded, and prayed he would not. It would mean another inquisition, nearly on the heels of the last one. She needed time to plan and create answers for the questions he would ask. She wasted no time, once the door was closed. A moment's hesitation might cause her to doubt the wisdom of what she had done so far. And that doubt would lead to weakness, and eventual doom. Had not bitter experience taught her that only the strong survived?

She would be strong, even if it meant that she would not be happy. She went to the bedside candle and lit it, carrying it to the little table in front of the window, where she was sure it could be seen from a distance.

It was still burning when she left the room for dinner.

Chapter Three

Will was beginning to fear that Penny had been correct in her suggestion that he use a Bath chair. If he lacked the strength to walk across his own room, there was no way he could manage the stairs to the ground floor without help from the servants. If he had to stagger to get down them, it would take all his energy to avoid the indignity of being carried back upstairs after.

As if it was not enough to lose memory and strength, he seemed prone to nerves—he started at the least little thing. He'd lain in bed, straining to hear the conversation in the hall, as Penny assured the mysterious Justine that everything would be fine. As he'd done so, he was overcome with the fear that the family was plotting against him, with the stranger. Even the entrance of his valet, with clean linen and shaving gear, set his heart to pounding. He'd been so sure of himself, before. Perhaps the blow had addled his brain, and the confidence would never return.

He refused to believe it. He would not spend the rest of his life hiding in his room and starting at shadows. If he worked to make it so, his life might be as it once was.

But now, he had a wife.

He did not wish to think of her, either. After he'd composed himself, it was a comfort to see his valet, Stewart. It was good to be clean, shaved and dressed in something other than a nightshirt. But it embarrassed him that he'd had to be helped into a sitting position and moved about like a mannequin when his limbs would not stay steady enough to help with trousers and coat.

His man had made no comment on it, other than to examine his cheek and remark that her ladyship was nearly as good with a razor as he, and might have made an excellent valet, had God blessed her enough to make her male.

'She shaved me?' Why did it bother him to imagine that graceful hand holding the blade to his throat?

Stewart smiled. 'She did everything for you, my lord. She was so attentive that all breathed a sigh of relief when she was not in the room. We feared she would exhaust herself with the effort.'

The man had said *all* as though he referred to both servants and family. It seemed that everyone in the house was taken with the love and dedication that the mysterious Justine had brought to her nursing. 'What else do the servants say of my new wife?' If there was any below-stairs gossip, Stewart would know of it. Hopefully, he owed enough loyalty to his master to give an honest opinion.

The man broke out in a grin. 'She is quite the finest woman in Wales, my lord. Gentle and kind, with a way about her that makes all in the household easy about the change. She has not spent much time with us, as yet. Your brother deemed it easier to keep you here than in your own home.' Will smiled to himself. For the first time in the discussion, there was the slightest hint of disapproval, and it was because a duke had the gall to overrule his servants in doing what was best for him.

Stewart was smiling again. 'We shall soon have you back with us, now that you are better, and all will be right again. And we shall have her ladyship as well.' The smile grew even broader, as though this addition was not so much a bother as the candied violet on top of a sweet.

Very well, then. All of Wales adored his wife. Logic dictated that he should as well. Had it not been pleasant to see her face, to hear her voice and to feel her gentle touch as he awoke? If he was still whole in body, he should have found it arousing to think that this lovely creature was familiar with the most intimate features of his anatomy. Those soft white hands had touched him as a lover, even as he'd lain helpless.

'Be careful, my lord.' His shudder at the thought had brought a caution from Stewart, whose scissors hovered near to Will's ear as the hair around it was trimmed.

Will took a deep breath and steadied himself. 'That is my intention, Stewart. From now on, I will be very careful, indeed.'

Despite the difficulties involved, Will took supper in the dining room with the family. Though his legs were still too watery to hold him, he could not stand the thought of a meal on a bed tray. Nor could he repress the nagging suspicion that if he was absent, he would be the main topic of conversation. On his way to the ground floor, he held tight to the stair rail and managed to ward off the sudden vertigo as he walked. A footman supported his other arm. While crossing the hall, he'd tried and rejected a walking stick, for his arms were not strong enough to hold it. By God, he would practise in his room, all day if necessary. He would be himself again.

Once he was seated at the dinner table, he felt almost normal. He'd practised sitting up in a chair until he was sure he was steady. And while he might not have an appetite for all the courses, he was still damned hungry. According to Stewart, they'd been giving him nothing but gruel from a pap cup for weeks. The very act of holding knife and fork was enough to raise his spirits, though the use of them was problematic.

It was after dropping yet another bite of fish, as he tried to guide it to his mouth, that he realised the hush that had fallen over the table. They were all watching him intently, as he ate.

He threw his fork aside. 'It is not any easier, when one is being stared at, you know.'

'Perhaps, if I were to cut your...' The woman, Justine, was leaning towards his plate, ready to slice his food as though he were too young to manage it himself.

'Certainly not,' he barked at her. In response, there was a nervous shifting of the other diners and his brother cleared his throat, as though to remind Will of his manners.

'I am sorry,' he grumbled. He was annoyed with her offer and even more so with himself for behaving like a lout. 'It is difficult.'

'Soon it will be easier,' she promised and signalled a footman, whispering a request.

With that, another course appeared, just for him. A ragout of beef had been poured into a tankard and there was a soft bit of bread as well. It was peasant fare and his table manners were a match for it. His hands shook as he brought the mug to his mouth and he wiped away any spillage with the bread. It embarrassed him to be so careless. But the others at table seemed so happy that he could eat at all, they ignored the manner of it and conversation returned to normal.

He could feel his strength returning with each bite. By the time he had finished, his hands had stopped shaking and he felt warm and comfortably full inside. Though it annoyed him to have to do so, he gave Justine a brief nod of thanks.

In response, she gave a modest incline of her head as if saying it was her honour to serve him. He might not know what to make of her sudden appearance in his life, but she seemed to feel no such confusion. Though she barely looked at him over dinner, she was ever aware of his needs and quick to see them tended to. The moment she'd realised his problem, she had moved to help him, while allowing him some small amount of dignity.

Would it be so bad to find that he had married a beauty willing to devote her life to his health and happiness? Tonight, she was wearing a dinner gown of moss-green silk. It might have seemed dull on another woman, but it brought out the colour of her eyes. The cut was lower than her day dress had been, but still quite modest. While it revealed a graceful neck and smooth shoulders, the hint of bosom visible made a man wonder all the more about the rest of her. And on her head was the same starched cap from the afternoon, hiding most of her curled hair.

It was hardly fair that he could not remember knowing her before she'd put on the modest trappings of marriage and covered her head. His brother's wife rarely bothered with such things. But that was less from a desire to display her white-blonde hair and more from a total uninterest in fashion.

In Justine's case, such attire felt less like modesty and more like a desire to hide something that he most wanted to see. It was the same for her pretty eyes that were cast down at her food instead of looking at him, and her beautiful voice, which did not speak unless spoken to. She was like a closed book, careful not to reveal too much. She stayed so quiet and still until the dessert was cleared away. Then she offered a curtsy and retired to the sitting room with Penny, leaving the men alone with their port.

'Can you manage the glass?' Adam asked, pouring for them both, 'or will it be too difficult?'

'For your cellars, I will make the effort,' Will said, wanting nothing more than a stiff drink to relieve the tension.

'See that you do not snap my head off, if you fail,' his brother added with a smile. 'Your wife may not mind it, but if I have any more trouble out of you I will call for the governess to put you to bed like your infant nephew.'

'Sorry,' Will said, still not feeling particularly apologetic. 'I have the devil of a megrim.' He frowned. 'But do not call for laudanum. If, as you say, I have been asleep for months, I do not relish the thought of drugged slumber tonight.'

'If?' Adam looked at him with arched eyebrows and took a sip of his drink. 'Tell me, William. You have known me all your life. In that time, have I ever lied to you?'

'Of course not,' he said, staring down into his drink and feeling foolish for sounding so sceptical. Then he added, 'But I have known you, on occasion, to believe the lies of others.'

Adam nodded. 'Who do you think is lying to me now? And how could they have managed, against such clear-cut evidence? I have watched you insensible in that bed upstairs for nearly two months. There was no question about the severity of your injury, or your nearness to death.'

'But you were not there at the time of the accident,' he prodded.

'No,' Adam agreed, 'I was not.'

'And you believe the story told by this Justine de Bryun?'

'Yes, I believe her story,' Adam replied. 'But her name is Lady Justine Felkirk. Because she is your wife.'

'How do you know that?' Will slammed his fist down on the table in frustration, making the crystal glasses shudder. I know that you were not at the wedding. 'Have you seen the licence?'

Adam did not hesitate. 'You married in Gretna, just as I did. No licence was necessary.'

'Then why do you believe her?' Will pressed him. 'What evidence do you have, other than the word of this stranger? How do you know that she is not responsible for the state I am in?'

His brother responded with a quelling look and said, 'Because I can find no reason to explain why she would injure you, then arrive at my home, exhausted from days spent in a coach, cradling your broken head in her lap, so that she might nurse you back to health.'

'Perhaps she is not at fault,' Will admitted, feeling even more foolish. 'But that does not mean I married her. If I experienced a grand passion that moved me to act so rashly as to wed, I would hope to feel some residue of it.'

'Residue?' Adam was smiling now. 'You speak of love as if it were a noxious mould.'

'Is it natural that I should forget a woman who looks like that?' Even his happily married brother must have noticed that Justine de Bryun was a beauty worthy of memory. 'Is it normal that I feel nothing, when I look at her?'

'Nothing?' his brother said in surprise.

Will shrugged. That last had not been precisely true. There was not a man alive who could look at his alleged wife and feel nothing. But surely he should not feel such a strange mix of suspicion and desire.

'Nothing about these last few months have been natural,' his brother said as though that explanation would be any comfort. 'But I can tell you that the one thing we have all grown to count on, since you were returned to us in such an unfortunate condition, was the love of your Justine. She never wavered in her loyalty to you, no matter how unlikely recovery seemed.'

'I do not fault her for her devotion,' Will said. 'But a compassionate stranger might have done the same for me.'

'She is more than that to you, I am sure,' Adam said. 'Once we knew her, I could not help but love her, as I am sure you did. She is not simply devoted and beautiful, she is talented as well. Good company, well mannered, the very opposite of the sort of empty-headed chits that sought you out in London.'

'It is all well and good that you love her,' Will reminded him. 'But you have a wife of your own.'

'Do not be an idiot,' Adam said with a snort. 'Penny loves her as well. They are practically sisters. In two months she has become like a member of our family.'

'That does not explain why I married her,' Will announced. 'Nor does it explain why you were willing to take her into the house with such a sham story as the one she brought. Sudden elopements? Riding accidents? That does not sound at all plausible. Have you ever known me to make major decisions on a whim? Do I drink to excess, bet foolishly, race my horses, or take up with strange women?'

'You are the most sensible of men,' Adam agreed. 'Almost too sensible to be a younger brother. It is I who should be lecturing you. I remember the way you scolded me, when I brought Penny to London…'

'Let us not speak of it,' Will said, holding up a hand. 'I was wrong. But as you say, I am almost too cautious. That is why I doubt the events as they have been presented to me. It is totally out of character for me to behave in such a way as Justine de Bryun ascribes to me. And you have only her word for the truth of it.'

Adam frowned and then admitted, 'We did doubt, at first. But once we knew her, all doubts were gone.'

'For what reason?' Will said, frustrated almost to anger.

'Because once we had spoken to her, it was clear she was exactly the sort of woman you'd have chosen for yourself. She is level-headed, wise, calm in adversity and has a quick wit. Her tastes and opinions, her sense of humour, and the hours she keeps? All are a perfect match to yours.' Adam shook his head in amazement. 'She is obviously your soul's mate, Will. How could you have married anyone else?'

'You cannot be serious,' he said. He thought back to his interactions with the girl, who would barely look him in the eye, much less speak aloud, and wondered if that was truly what others saw in him.

Adam smiled. 'I know it is difficult, at the moment, But you must have seen these qualities yourself, when you met her. It was clearly a matter of like attracting like. Trust me, Will. More accurately, the two of you are like iron and a lodestone. She has been nearly inseparable from you since the first moment she arrived. She allows herself a brief walk each morning, but other than that, she was never far from your side.'

'Except at night,' Will added. The thought of such constant scrutiny felt almost oppressive.

'Most nights, she slept on a cot in your dressing room,' Adam said. 'She wanted to be near if you awakened. There was no part of your care too lowly that she would not at least attempt it.'

There was that thrill of fear again, that he had felt as he'd thought of her holding a razor. She was certainly as lovely as Delilah. Could she not be as dangerous as well?

But it seemed that Adam had no such worries. 'She has worked, from the first, as though she already possessed your love and admiration. I am sure you will find it again, once you are fully recovered. In the mean time, if you cannot trust your own heart, trust your family. All will be well. Now finish your drink and let me help you to your room. No doubt you will feel differently in the morning.'

And when had he ever trusted his heart when making such a momentous decision? As Adam shepherded him up the stairs, there was no point in telling him the futility of that advice. The heart was a capricious organ, likely to say the opposite of his poor dented skull. As his valet helped him prepare for bed, he still felt headachy and weak, and utterly confused. He did not dare tell Stewart, or even his brother, that, now that it was dark, he dreaded returning to the bed he had lain in for so long. Suppose he closed his eyes and opened them to discover that he had lost another half a year?

Surely that would not happen. He had improved since the afternoon. While the pain and confusion remained, the blank slate of his memory had begun to fill again, even if the scrawls he imagined on it were written in someone else's hand. Now, he must sleep, even though he did not feel tired. In the morning, he would walk, though he had no real desire to move. Little by little he would fight off the stupor and force body and mind to function at his command.

Stewart departed and there was the softest of

knocks on the door. Without waiting for his answer, Justine entered, silent as a ghost in her plain linen nightdress.

And here was another appetite that had nothing to do with the condition of heart or mind. When he looked at Justine, desire did not need memory, just the evidence of his eyes. Her body would be soft and warm under the fall of thin white cloth and she would press it to his, should he demand it of her. They could dispense with the gown entirely and the ridiculous nightcap she wore with it. And for a time, he would forget any fears of past or future and revel in a glorious present. Perhaps a repeat of what they had already done would jar some knowledge in him.

Or would it be as feared? Even after a night together, she might be as much an enigma as she was now? There was something disquieting in those deep-green eyes and that placid smile. It was like a beautiful mask that could come off at midnight and reveal something totally unexpected.

The thought of bedding her had him as nervous as a bridegroom. If the stories were true, he had been that once already. On that night, his body would have performed as he commanded it to. If he was too weak to walk unaided, how was he to manage with a woman in his bed? Would she measure him against previous experience?

Perhaps she had fears as well. She looked rather like a virgin sacrifice in the undecorated white gown with her hair, a touchable river of gold, flowing down her back in a loose braid. In the firelight, she seemed younger than he'd thought, no more than two and twenty.

It made him feel strangely guilty to have suspected her of anything. She looked too innocent to be harbouring some dark secret. There was nothing in her demeanour that said she looked forward to a physical reunion with him. Now that they were alone again, the shyness he had seen at dinner was all the more noticeable.

Then, suspicion returned. If she was truly his wife, should she not be more excited to find him awake and alive, and to renew the physical relationship between them? Perhaps he had married her and discovered the ardour he felt was not returned. She had called him good, and kind, before. But she had not spoken of desire, or hung about his neck showering him with relieved kisses. The smile she gave him now was pleasant, but cool.

The one he returned to her was tight and unwillingly given. 'What are you doing here?' he said, not bothering to hide his doubts.

'I thought, now that you were awake…'

Did she think that she would climb into bed with him and make everything better? That they would rut busily for a time, for no other reason than to prove that his lack of past did not affect either of them? Were men really so easily manipulated as that?

She walked past him and sat on the opposite edge of his bed, perched like a perfectly formed wooden doll on the very edge of a shelf. If he touched her, she would fall on to her back with that same distant look in her eyes, spread her legs and let him do as he wished with her.

The thought made him feel strangely sick. A little awkwardness after all this time would not be unusual. If the couple were in love, it might be laughed away after a whispered conversation on the need for patience and the assurance that nothing mattered more than their time together.

But he could not imagine having such a talk with her. When he looked at Justine, he felt nothing but a vague, unsettling desire. He wanted to see what lay under that prim gown she was wearing as much as he'd wanted to see under the cap and touch her hair. Most of all, he wanted to come inside her, feeling the past return in a rush, turning the past day into nothing more than a horrible dream.

But what did she want? She was gazing at him with a look of placid acceptance that was not encouraging. Perhaps proper women did not take pleasure in the marital bed. If they did not, then what real joy could there be to lie with her? He envied Adam and Penny, so obviously two sides of the same coin. Perhaps that was not what was meant to be for him. Adam had said he and this woman were alike. If she was cold and apathetic, what did that make him?

He had gone too long, staring at her without answer. So she started again. 'While you were ill, I never slept far from your room. I have a cot, in the dressing room. In case you cried out in your sleep, I wanted to be nearby.'

'That will no longer be necessary,' he said. It was probably meant to be a comfort, but he wanted nothing more than to be alone, to puzzle out what had happened to him.

She bit her lip. 'I wish to remain close, should you need me. But as my husband, it is up to you to decide where you wish me to be.' She glanced significantly at the bed beside her. It was the only moment of spirit in her too-perfect subservience.

It made him want to bed her even less. He remained blank for a moment more. Then he gave a laugh of mock surprise. 'I am sorry to inform you of this, my dear, but it does not matter to me in the least where you wish to sleep tonight. I am far too tired to manage anything so strenuous as a loving reunion.'

As he had feared, she looked more relieved than disappointed by his refusal. She stood up mechanically and turned first towards the hall, then towards the door that led to a connecting bedroom. 'Then I will return to my room and leave you to your rest. If you need anything in the night…'

'I shall ring for a servant,' he said firmly. 'You do not need to trouble yourself any further, or sleep at the foot of my bed like a hound. If I need you specifically, I shall walk across the room and knock upon your door.'

A certain type of woman might have snapped at his rudeness, or burst into a torrent of foolish tears.

This one gave him an impassive nod and answered as a servant would, 'Very good, my lord.'

A nagging voice at the back of his head demanded that he stop being foolish. Even if they were not two halves of one heart, it gave him no reason to treat her like a footman. 'I will see you in the morning,' he said, trying to use a kinder tone. 'In the breakfast room.'

'Of course.' And once he saw her there, would she eat when he told her, drink when he told her and in all other ways behave like an automaton? If so, it did not matter what Adam thought. Justine was the exact opposite of the wife he would have wanted. There was no spirit in her at all, no challenge. There was nothing in her to learn, no exciting discoveries to make. The woman leaving his room was perfectly beautiful, totally obedient and dull.

Then he was rewarded with a fleeting memory of the past. He had been watching Adam at the christening, who was full of pride over his son and his duchess. The boy had been crying and his mother near to panic at her inability to maintain order. But Adam could not have looked happier. The room had seemed almost too full of life. For the first time in his life, Will had found something to envy. He had wanted a wife. And he had, indeed, resolved to marry within the year.

The fact that he could not remember bringing it about was a moot point. The thought had been in his mind when he left the house. He was going south. There were any number of fashionable women who would welcome his offer, now that he had decided to make it. He would choose one of them, after…

After what? There had been something else he'd meant to do. Only afterwards had he intended to marry. He must have achieved his goal, whatever it was. He had carried out the second part of his plan and found a wife.

Now, he would have to make the best of his choice. He leaned over to blow out the candle settling back into a bed that was familiar, but strangely empty.

Chapter Four

In the weeks she'd spent at Bellston Manor, Justine had come up with a dozen excuses for her early morning walks. She enjoyed regular exercise. She had a love of the outdoors. She wished to become familiar with the area that would be her home, after the unlikely recovery of William Felkirk. She had caught Penny and the duke discussing her regular exercise with approval. They had been nodding sagely to each other about the need for poor Justine to escape the sickroom, even for a short period of time.

It pained her that they were so willing to accept what was nothing more than another lie. There was only one reason that truly mattered. In a regular series of lonely rambles, it was easy to disguise the few times she did not walk alone.

It took nearly ten minutes to cross the manicured park around the great house. Beyond that, the path wound into the trees and she was hidden from view.

Most mornings, the concealment gave her the chance to let down her guard and be truly herself. That brief time amongst the oaks was all hers and it was a novelty. How many years had it been since she had called her life her own, even for a moment?

But this was not most mornings. Today, the privacy meant nothing more than a change of façades. She was barely concealed before she heard the step behind her. Even though she had been expecting it, she started at the sudden appearance of John Montague.

That he invariably startled her was a source of annoyance. He made no effort to blend with the wood or the countryside. He wore the same immaculately tailored black coats and snowy white breeches he favoured in town. The patterned silk of his waistcoats stood out like a tropical bird lost amongst the trees. His heavy cologne was devoid of woodsy notes. His body and face were sharp and angular, his complexion florid to match his wiry red hair.

The only subtlety he possessed was his ability to move without a sound. Whether walking through the leaves, or over the hard marble of the jewellery shop they ran in Bath, she never heard the click of a heel or the shuffle of a foot to mark his approach. Like a cat, he was suddenly there, at one's side, and then he would be gone. After each meeting she spent hours, starting at nothing and glancing nervously over her shoulder, convinced that he might be nearby, listening, watching, waiting to pounce.

As usual, he laughed at her fear as though it gave him pleasure. Then he pulled her forward, into his arms to remind her that it was not William Felkirk to whom she belonged. She permitted his kiss, as she always did, remaining placid. If one could not summon a response other than revulsion, it was best to show no emotion at all. When she could stand no more of it, she pulled away, pretending that it was the urgent need to share information that made her resist his advances.

He cocked his head to the side as though trying to decide whether it was worth punishing her for her impudence. Then he spoke. 'I saw the light in your window. You have news?'

'Felkirk is awake.'

Montague gave a sharp intake of breath and she hurried to add, 'But he remembers nothing.'

'Nothing?' He smiled at this miraculous turn of events.

'Not a thing from the last six months,' she assured him. 'He does not remember his investigations. He does not remember you.' *Nor me*, she added to herself. 'Most importantly, he does not remember the injury. I told him it was a riding accident.'

'Did he believe you?' Montague said, with no real optimism.

'I do not know.'

'What will happen if circumstances change?'

'It will be a disaster,' she said. 'I must be gone before then.' Her plan to escape Montague was an utter failure, if she must run back to him now. But better to return to the devil she knew than to experience what might happen should Lord Felkirk remember the truth.

'What of the diamonds?' Montague asked. 'You have been in the house for weeks. Am I to believe you found nothing?'

'Not a thing,' she admitted.

'Did you examine the Duchess's jewel case?'

Justine sighed. 'Have I not told you so already? I feigned feminine curiosity and she showed me all. There are no stones in any of the pieces that match the ones my father was carrying.'

'They must be hidden elsewhere.' Montague insisted. 'When he came to Bath, Felkirk was sure he'd found the hiding place.'

'Then the information is locked in his brain along with the reason for his condition.' Justine resisted the urge to tug upon his arm, to lead him further from the house. He seemed to think even the most innocent contact between them gave him permission to take further liberties. 'You must get me away from here,' she said.

Montague grunted in disgust. 'But we will not have the diamonds. Without them, we have gained nothing from this little game you suggested. You might just as well have let me finish him, while we were still in Bath.'

'Suppose he had told someone of his plans?' She took the risk of stroking his arm to distract him.

'Isn't it better to know that there is no trail leading back to you?'

'You discovered that almost immediately,' he retorted. 'If there were no diamonds to find, then you should have done as I suggested and smothered him while he slept.'

'You know I could not,' she said, as calmly as possible. To hear him speak so casually of cold-blooded murder made her tremble. Even knowing that her life might be at stake, she could not bring herself to do such a thing.

'I fail to see what stops you,' Montague replied. 'His family was responsible for the death of your father, who was my closest friend.' He beat his breast once to emphasise the connection. 'He was murdered on their property, delivering stones for a necklace that the duchess did not give two figs for. They did not keep their land safe for travellers. They did not offer a guard to escort him to the house. And once the crime had occurred they made no effort to catch the killer. Even worse, they may have been complicit. If Felkirk is right and the stones are still on the property, what are we to believe?'

'I doubt that is the case,' she said. It made no sense. What reason would a duke have to rob a jewel merchant, when they could easily afford to pay for the stones?

'Perhaps not,' Montague allowed. 'But some justice is owed, after all this time.'

'True,' she said, cautiously. 'But it was very dangerous to take that justice into your own hands by attacking the brother of the duke.' Had her father known there was this strain of madness in his part-ner, when he'd made him guardian to a pair of help-less orphans? It did not matter, for there was little she could do about it until Margot was of age. 'Since he survived the attack and cannot remember what oc-curred, you will be safe from prosecution.'

'All well and good,' he said. 'But when you sug-gested this ruse, you promised you would find the diamonds Felkirk was searching for and bring them to me.'

It had surprised her that he would believe such a thing. If she had uncovered the stones her father had lost, her plan had been to sell them and escape with her sister to a place where neither Montague nor Fel-kirk could find her. 'As I've told you before, I can find no evidence of them. The plan is a failure. You must help me quit this house, before it is too late and Lord Felkirk remembers who I am.' Then she sighed and offered herself as an incentive. 'We might take a room at an inn on the road back to Bath.'

'Do you miss me?' he asked, with a smile that made her shiver. 'How flattering. Do not worry. You will return to my bed soon enough, and it will be just as it was before Felkirk sought us out. But I think, for a time, you had best remain where you are. His memory might return. Perhaps you can coax forth the information we need and we will still succeed.'

'It will require me to convince him that I am his

wife,' she said. 'You know what he will expect from me.' She held her breath, praying that Montague's possessiveness would finally do her some good.

He grabbed her by the arm and she thought he meant to punish her for even suggesting such a thing. But then he kissed her, forcing his tongue into her open mouth, thrusting hard, as though the idea of her laying with another excited him. Or perhaps he meant to frighten her into submission.

That would have been pointless. She had learned, at times like this, to feel nothing at all. She had but to wait and it would be over, soon enough.

Eventually, he pulled away and whispered, 'You must use your talents on him, my dear. I swear you are woman enough to give speech to a dead man. How hard will it be for you to turn Felkirk inside out and extract what you need from him?'

'But suppose I cannot?' she said. 'Suppose he remembers seeing me with you. In Bath, I am sure he guessed I was your mistress. I could see it in his eyes. Do not make me do this, for it is sure to fail.'

'You had best see that it does not,' he said. 'For your own sake and your sister's.'

'Do not mention Margot again,' she said, yanking her arm free from his grasp as the fear he wanted to see flooded back into her.

'I will speak of her, or to her, whenever I wish.' He knew her weakness and exploited it, relishing her reaction. 'Until she is of age, Margot is still my ward.' Then he took her hand back, more gently this time, running his fingers along the skin in a way he must think would excite her. 'Without you, my life is so very lonely, Justine. Perhaps I should bring Margot home from school. She could take your place, working in the shop. She could keep me company, until you return.' He raised her hand to his lips, running the tip of his tongue along the knuckles. 'I swear, she is very nearly as lovely as you.'

Her mind went blank again, blocking out the feeling of his lips touching her skin. 'It will not be necessary to summon Margot,' she said, in a calm, agreeable voice. 'I will do exactly as you say. I will discover what it is that Felkirk found. Then, I will return to you and things will be just as they were.'

'See that you do,' he said, looking up into her eyes. 'You are to do whatever is necessary to gain the knowledge we want. I will have those stones, Justine. And then I will have you back.'

Whatever was necessary. She would lie to William Felkirk and lie with him as well. Perhaps there would still be a way to find the diamonds and get away. But until then, she would lose a little bit of herself, just as she did each time with Montague. How much was left to lose, when one already felt empty? 'Of course,' she agreed, listening to the sound of her own voice as if it came from a great distance. She thought of Margot and the need for her to stay safe at school, and innocent, for just one more year. 'I will do whatever is necessary.'

Then she let Montague kiss her again, making her

mind a blank as the kiss grew more passionate. But now he was pulling her away from the path, deeper into the woods so that they could be alone. There was no time for it.

She pushed him away and straightened her dress. 'They expect me back at the house. It was only to be a short walk. I will be missed if I tarry. And if Felkirk comes down to breakfast, he will want to see me there.' Then she kissed Montague once, gently on the mouth, hoping that he would believe she was not simply avoiding him.

'Of course,' he agreed, smoothing her hair and straightening her bonnet for another excuse to touch her. 'Go back to the house. Do not arouse suspicion. But do not take too long about it. Remember, Margot is coming home for Christmas. If you cannot be with us, I will send your love…'

She turned and hurried back to the house, surprised, as she always was, at the way that her guardian could turn a simple, parting phrase into a threat.

Chapter Five

Will slept uneasily, waking often and with a start, as though proving to himself that it was truly possible to open his eyes again. But by morning, the ache in his head had diminished. He was able to take a few shaky steps around the room before calling for the crutches that the servants had found, to help him.

In the breakfast room, he found other servants, already clearing away a plate that still held a half-eaten slice of toast slathered with the marmalade from Tim Colton's orangery. It was his particular favourite. The pot on the table was half-empty.

His brother barely looked up from his coffee. 'If you are looking for your wife, she is up and out of the house already. She favours a morning walk, much as you do when you are in the country.'

'Oh.' He stared out the window at the fading green of the park and the coloured leaves swirling in the breeze. 'That particular habit will be quite beyond me for a time.'

Adam nodded, then smiled. 'You have no idea how good it is to see you on your feet again, even if you are a trifle unsteady.'

'Probably not,' Will agreed. 'For me, it is as if no time has passed at all.'

'It is a blessing, then,' Adam said. 'You do not remember the pain.'

'That is not all I have lost,' Will reminded him, glancing at the marmalade pot.

'And as I told you, there is nothing to fear. Unlike my own darling Penelope, Justine is the most patient of women. She will not be hurt by your forgetfulness.'

'I had not thought of that,' Will said. If he had married her, then the hardship was not all on one side.

Adam looked even more surprised. 'How inconsiderate of you. While you were the one who was injured, there were others who bore the brunt of the pain and worry. And over something so uncharacteristically foolish as a fall from a horse.'

'Exactly,' Will said. 'What would have caused me to do such a thing?'

'Showing off for Justine, I expect,' Adam said, moderating his voice to sound less like a scold. 'All men are idiots, when they are in love.'

On this, Will agreed. 'That is why I have always avoided being so.'

'Until now,' Adam finished.

'And that is one more thing I do not understand,' Will said, feeling more desperate than he had before. 'You claim she is just like me. Perhaps it is true.

But why did I not take the time to bring her home to meet you, and to marry properly, in a church? If she is so like me, why did she not insist on it? It is not reasonable.'

His brother laughed. 'You cannot think of a single reason to marry such a woman in haste? You poor fellow.'

'She is pretty, of course,' he allowed.

'Was your vision affected?' Adam asked, drily. 'She is a damn sight more than just pretty.'

'A beauty, then,' Will admitted reluctantly. 'But the world is full of those and I have resisted them all.'

'Until now,' his brother replied.

'But I have no clue as to what caused this magical change in me? And what took me to Bath?'

Adam frowned. 'It will come back to you in time, I'm sure. If not, you can ask Justine.' Adam gave him a searching look. 'You have spoken to her, haven't you?'

'Briefly,' Will admitted.

'Which means that you have exchanged fewer words with her than you have with me.'

William shook his head. 'I would rather hear your version of events first.'

'You will find her story is much the same as mine,' Adam said. 'While you cannot remember her, there is no reason to assume that she will not be forthcoming if you ask these questions of her.'

Will paused, unsure of how to explain himself. Then he said, 'It is not just that I have forgotten our marriage. I have the strangest feeling that she is not to be trusted.'

Adam stifled an oath before mastering his patience. 'The physicians told us that you might be prone to dark moods, if you recovered at all. Do not let yourself be ruled by them.'

'Suppose I cannot prevent it?' he said in return. 'You claim I will love her as I once did, given time. Suppose I do not?'

'Then I would assume that you are not fully recovered from your injury and tell you that even more time was required.' Adam seemed to think it was much less complicated than it seemed to him.

'Then you must ready your advice,' Will replied. 'For when I look at her, I do not love her, nor can I imagine a time when I did.'

Adam sighed. 'You always did lack imagination.'

'Perhaps that is true. But I do not wish to develop it, simply to create a likely scenario for my previous marriage. If I cannot remember her, would an annulment not be a possibility? Surely a mental deficiency on my part...'

Adam's eyes narrowed. 'There is no sign that you were mentally defective when you met her. The accident happened afterwards. A declaration of mental deficiency on your part would cause other problems as well. Do you wish me to take on the management of your money and land, since you are clearly unable to make decisions for yourself? Will you seek to marry again? How will we guarantee to the next woman that she will not meet a similar fate? Unless you want to be declared my ward for the rest of your life and treated as though you cannot manage your own affairs, you had best own what wits you have.'

Will had no answer to this.

'Far better that you should meet your wife as if she were a stranger and grow to feel for her again. I suspect the answer to it all is quite unexceptional. Standing up at the christening put you in mind to marry. You went to Bath, where you knew many young ladies were to be found, chose the most likely candidate and made your offer. Since you were so adamantly opposed to my own sudden marriage, when it happened, you would not have entered into a similar union had the bond between you not been strong.'

It sounded right. But Will still could not manage to believe it. 'What if I was driven by some other reason?'

'Then I would tell you, if you cannot love her, there is nothing about her that is unlikeable. She is beautiful, talented and quite devoted to you. Many marriages are built on less. You could do worse than to keep her.' Adam was using the matter-of-fact tone he used when settling disputes amongst the tenants. It was the sort of voice that said there would be no further discussion.

So the decision was already made. He was married. His brother did not seem to care if he wanted to be. Nor could Will explain the nagging feeling, at the back of his mind, that something was very wrong with this. 'How am I to go about growing this feeling? What advice do you have, oh, wise Bellston?'

Adam gave a confident smile. 'I would advise that you find your wife immediately, and spend the day with her. Then you must remove yourself from my household as soon as you are able.'

'You are turning me out?' Will said with surprise. 'I am barely recovered.'

'Your own home is less than a mile from here,' Adam said with a calming gesture. 'The doctor is even closer to that place than he is to here. It is not that you are not welcome to visit. But the sooner you stop making excuses and isolate yourself with Justine, the sooner you will come to love her again. The pair of you must stop using the rest of us to avoid intimacy.'

'You expect me to bed a complete stranger, hoping that I will rise in the morning with my love renewed?'

He could see by the narrowing of his brother's eyes that Adam was nearly out of patience. 'Perhaps the bump on the head has truly knocked all sense out of you. You talk as if it were a hardship to lie with a beautiful woman. But I meant nothing so vulgar. You must be alone with her. Talk. Share a quiet evening or two and discover what it was that drew you to her in the first place. I predict, before the week is out, you will be announcing your complete devotion to her.'

'Very well, then. Today I will discuss the matter with her. Tomorrow, I will take her home, and make some effort to treat her as if she were a wife by my choice. But I predict we will be having the same conversation in a week's time. Then I will expect you to offer something more substantive than empty platitudes about love.'

So he finished his breakfast and, with his brother's words in mind, sought out Justine. But she seemed no more eager to talk to him than he was to talk to her. The servants informed him that, directly after her walk, she'd gone out with the duchess to call on the sick and needy of the village.

Penny returned without her. It seemed she had been invited to luncheon with the vicar, to celebrate the miraculous recovery of his invalid husband. That they had neglected to invite Will to the event was an oversight on their part.

By afternoon, she had returned to the house, though Will could not manage to find her. When he went to visit his nephew in the nursery, he was told that the boy was just down for a nap. Her ladyship had sung him to sleep. The nurse assured him his wife had the voice of an angel and was naturally good with children. Apparently he had chosen the perfect mother for his future brood, should he find it in his heart to make them with her.

It was hard to accuse her of dark motives when she seemed to fill her day with virtues. It explained why his family was so taken with her. But to Will, it seemed almost as if she was deliberately avoiding him. Wherever he went in the house, her ladyship had just been and gone, after doing some kindness or proving her own excellent manners.

In the end, he did not see her until supper, after they had both dressed for it on opposite sides of the connecting door. Adam was entertaining the Coltons, claiming it as a small celebration welcoming him back to health. More likely, it was an attempt to put Will on his best behaviour. Tim and Daphne were old family friends. But that did not give him the right to bark and snap at them, as he had been doing with his own family.

At least this evening he was able to manage food and drink without subtle aid from his new wife. Though he was fatigued, a single day out of bed and a few hearty meals had worked wonders on his depleted body.

As the conversation droned on about Tim's latest experiments in his greenhouse, Will lifted his glass and looked through it, across the table at the woman he supposedly loved. Today, her gown was white muslin shot through with gold threads, her warm gold hair falling in inviting spirals from another dull white cap. But for that, she'd have looked like one of the more risqué angels in a Botticelli painting, pure but somehow a little too worldly.

She noticed his gaze and coloured sweetly, keeping her own eyes firmly focused on the food in front of her. Perhaps it was simply that he felt better today. Perhaps it was the wine. Or maybe leaving the confines of his room changed his mood. But he wondered what it was that had made him distrust her, when there was nothing exceptional in her behaviour.

She seemed shy of him, of course. But could she be blamed for it? Since the first moment he'd opened his eyes, she had shown him nothing but kindness and patience. He had responded with suspicion and hostility. Even a real angel would grow tired of such treatment and draw away.

Almost as an experiment, he looked directly at her, long past the point where she could ignore him. Slowly her face rose, to return a nervous smile, head tilted just enough to express enquiry. Then he smiled at her and gave the slightest nod of approval.

She held his gaze for only a moment, before casting her eyes down again. But there was a flicker of a smile in response and tension he had not noticed disappeared from her back and shoulders. If possible, she became even prettier. She was more alluring, certainly. She had seemed almost too prim and virginal, perching on the edge of her chair.

But as she relaxed, her body looked touchable, as though she was aware of the pleasures it offered. If he had been married to her for even one night, he knew them himself. He would not have been able to resist. But it was an odd contrast to the woman she had been last night. As she'd sat on his bed, near enough to touch and waiting for intimacy, she'd been as stiff as a waxwork and just as cold.

After the meal, he'd been hoping for a relaxing glass of port with Adam and Sam as the ladies retired. But they took that hurriedly, wanting to join the women in the parlour and using the comfort of the chairs, and his semi-invalid status, as an excuse. At first, he thought it a trick to throw him back into the presence of his wife and force some memory from him. But it seemed that, as their bachelor days receded into the past, his brother and friend had grown used to spending their evenings in the company of their wives. They were less willing to forgo it, even after his miraculous recovery. Now that he was married, they expected him to behave the same.

Married.

It always came back to that. Once again, his feelings were in a muddle. Perhaps he was still avoiding her. He should be able to engage Justine in easy conversation as Adam and Sam did with their wives. But he could not think of a word to say to her, other than the thought that was always foremost in his mind: *Who are you?*

No one else wondered. They all seemed to know her well. She was settled into what was probably her usual chair beside a screened candle, chatting amiably as though she belonged here. She reached into a basket at its side to take up her needlework: a complex arrangement of threads and pins on a satin pillow. The other women smiled at her, admired her work and discussed children and households.

Adam and Sam seemed to be in the middle of a political conversation that he'd had no part in. How long would it take him, just to be aware of the news of the day? Probably less time than to discover the details of his own life. He could read *The Times* for a day or two and find everything he needed. But no matter how he prodded at the veil covering the last six months, it was immovable. If the present situation was to be believed, there was a trip to Bath, love, marriage and who knew what other events, waiting just on the other side.

His headache was returning.

He struggled to his feet and manoeuvred himself to a decanter of brandy that sat on the table by the window, pouring a glass and drinking deeply. That he had done it without spilling a drop deserved a reward, so he poured a second, leaning on his crutches to marshal his strength for a return to his chair. The trip across the room had brought him scant feet from Justine and he paused to watch her work.

There was a scrap of lace, pinned flat to the pillow in front of her. It took him a moment to realise that this was not some purchased trim, but a work in progress. The finished work was held in place with a maze of pins more numerous than spines on a hedgehog, the working edge trailing away into a multitude of threads and dangling ivory spools. As though she hardly thought, she passed one over the other, around back, a second and a third, this time a knot, the next a braid. Then she slipped a pin into the finished bit and moved on to another set of threads. The soft click of ivory against ivory and the dance of her white hands were like a soporific, leaving him as calm as she seemed to be. Though he was close enough to smell her perfume, he saw no sign of the shyness that was usually present when he stood beside her. There was no stiffness or hesitation in the movement of her hands. Perhaps their problems existed outside the limits of her concentration. She worked without pattern, calling the complex arrangement of threads up from memory alone. There was hardly a pause in conversation, when one or the other of the women put a question to her. If it bothered her at all, he could not tell for her dancing fingers never wavered.

Though he stood right in front of her, he seemed to be the last thing on her mind. Now he felt something new when he looked at her. Was this envy that she gave her attention to the lace, and to the other women, while ignoring him? Or was this frustration that he'd had her attention, once, and slept through it.

Slowly, the roll of finished work at the top grew longer. No wonder she had nursed him, uncomplaining, for months at a time. She had the patience to measure success in inches. Penny noticed his interest and announced, 'Her handwork is magnificent.'

It brought a blush to the woman's fair cheeks, but she did not pause, or lose count of the threads. 'In my homeland, lacemaking is quite common,' she announced. 'My mother was far better at it than I.'

'Your homeland?' he prompted, for it was yet another fact that he did not know.

'Belgium,' she said, softly. 'I was born in Antwerp.'

'And we met in Bath,' he added. It did not answer how either of them came to be there. But perhaps, if repeated often enough, it would make sense.

'You may think it common, but your work is the most delicate I have seen,' Penny reminded her with a sigh. Then she looked to Will. 'It is a shame that you did not bring Justine to us before the last christening. I would so have liked to see a bonnet of that trim she is making now.'

'For the next child, you shall have one,' Justine replied, not looking up.

'It is too much to ask.' Penny smiled at Will as though he had a share in the compliment. 'The collar she made for me last month makes me feel as regal as a duchess.' Fine praise indeed, for it was rare to hear Penny feeling anything other than ordinary.

'The edging she made for my petticoat is so fine it seemed a shame to cover it with a skirt, Daphne added. 'I've had my maid take up the hem of the dress so that it might be seen to good advantage.'

'Because you are shameless,' her husband added with a smile. He was glancing at her legs as though there were other things that were too pretty to be hidden. It was probably true, if one had a taste for girls who were buxom and ginger. Daphne was as pretty as Penny was sensible.

Will glanced at his own wife, his mind still stumbling over the concept. The candlelight was shining copper in her hair and bringing out the green in her eyes. In museums, he'd admired the technique of the Flemish painters and the way their subject seemed to glow like opals in the light. But if this woman was an indication, perhaps they had simply learned to paint what they saw before them. Though she sat still and silent in the corner, the woman he had chosen seemed illuminated from within, like the banked coals of a fire. Perhaps that was what had drawn him to her. For now that he had seen her in candlelight, he could not seem to look away.

There was a knock on the parlour door and Adam all but leapt to his feet to open it, breaking the spell. He turned back to Will with a grin. 'Now, for the highlight of the evening. We are to have a visit from your namesake, William.' He opened the door and the nurse entered, carrying a plump toddler that Will assumed was his nephew.

It was almost as great a shock as discovering he had a wife. When he had last seen little William, they had been in the chapel and the infant had been squawking at the water poured over his head. That child had been but a few months old and had cared for nothing but milk and sleep. The baby that was brought into the room was fully three times the size of the one he remembered and struggling to escape, his arms outstretched to his parents, demanding their attention.

Penny had already set aside the book she'd been holding and took the baby, making little cooing noises and interrogating the nurse about his day. Next, it was Adam's turn. But instead of coddling the child, he knelt on the floor and demanded that his son come to him. The child did, once he was free of his mother's arms. It was done in a series of lunges, combined with some industrious crawling and ending in an impressive attempt by little Billy to haul himself upright on the leg of the tea table. He was properly rewarded by his father with a hug and a sweet that appeared from out of Adam's waistcoat pocket, which Penny announced would ruin the boy's sleep.

Will felt a strange tightening in his chest at the sight. Six months ago, he had given little thought to his nephew, other than a natural pride at sharing his name. But to have missed so much in the boy's development was like losing a thing he'd had no idea he'd wanted.

Adam scooped the child from the floor and wiped the stickiness from his hands and mouth before announcing, 'And now, young Bill, it is time to meet your uncle. Can you say hello for him? Come now,' he coaxed. 'We have heard the word before. Uncle. Show your godfather how brilliant you are.'

But as they approached, Billy showed no interest in speech. In fact, he'd wound his little hands tightly into his father's lapel and turned his face into the cloth. The closer they came, the more shy Billy seemed to become. By the time they were standing before Will, he could see nothing but the boy's hunched shoulders and curling blond hair.

'Hello, Bill,' he said softly, hoping that the boy was only playing a game with him. 'Peek-a-boo.'

Instead of laughing at the sound of his voice, the boy let out a scream and burst into tears, butting his head into his father's shoulder as though demanding to be taken away.

'I don't understand,' Adam said. 'He has seen you before. We took him to your room, each day. We would not have him forget...'

'It is all right,' Will said. But it was not. Had the time he'd lost turned him into a monster? What could the boy see that the others were not remarking on?

Now Penny was fussing over the child, taking him from Adam with a dark look. 'This is too much excitement. I will take him back to the nursery. It is time for bed, if it is possible to calm him.'

Will's head was pounding and the screaming boy was making it worse. 'No. I will go. Leave him be.' One crutch slipped out from under him for a moment and he nearly stumbled. But at least as he staggered it was in the direction of the hall. He allowed the momentum to carry him from the room, not bothering to shut the door behind him.

Chapter Six

Tere was a moment of shocked silence in the room, after William Felkirk's sudden retreat. Even the child was quiet, other than to heave a wet sigh of relief. And then all started for the door at once.

'I will go,' said Justine in as firm a voice as she could manage. Apparently, it was strong enough. Everyone relaxed. Even the duke took a step away from the door and offered an equally quiet, 'Of course. It must be you.'

She did not particularly want to follow, if it meant being alone with Lord Felkirk again. His refusal of her on the previous evening had come as a relief. She had half-feared, even before receiving Montague's orders, she might have to feign affection for a man she wanted no part of.

While nursing him, she had not bothered to think too much about the character of the man she was caring for. The feeding, washing and changing of linens had been little more than a series of tasks to be completed. It was good to be busy and to occupy her mind with the routine of duty.

But that was over now. Tonight, she might have to lie still in his bed, her own thoughts and fears clamouring loud in her head, while he did whatever he wished…

She had hoped for continued indifference, for at least a little while longer. If they could live as strangers for a while, she might think of some way to escape before the inevitable occurred. But he had been watching her, all during dinner, and in the parlour as she'd worked. And he had been smiling. Although it was better than his continual suspicion, it had been the sort of warm, speculative smile she had seen on the faces of men before. It was likely the first step in a chain of events that would lead to the bedroom and trap her even deeper in the lie she had told.

She put the fear of that aside as she went out into the hall. At the moment, he needed her. He needed someone, at least. His wife would be the logical choice to offer comfort. The poor man had quit the room like a wounded animal after his godson's rejection. Even with the complications it would add to her life, she could not abide the sight of suffering.

'Wait!' She needn't have called out after him. She caught him easily, for he'd had to struggle with the crutches and his own limited strength. He'd travelled as far as the end of the hall to the little, round mirror that hung there and was staring into it, as though expecting to see a monster.

She came to his side, allowing him to know her presence by her reflection. 'You must not think too much of that. Billy is normally the most agreeable of children. But even the best babies can take fright when they are startled.'

'Have I really changed so much?' Will touched his own face, as though doubting what he saw.

'Not really.' Much as she did not wish to admit it, he was even more handsome than he had been in Bath. His hair was as black as ever, except for the small streak of white near the scar. His skin, pale from illness, added to his dramatic good looks. And the easy smiles and relaxed manners he used at home were much less intimidating than the distant courtesy of the gentleman who had walked into the shop wishing to speak with Mr Montague about a crime committed in Wales nearly twenty years ago.

She had taken an instant dislike to him, for bringing up a subject that was still very painful to her. But amongst his family he seemed younger and more open. He had barely smiled at her and she had not yet seen him laugh. But she could see by the lines around his mouth and eyes that he did so, and frequently. He seemed like a most pleasant fellow. It was a shame to see him doubt himself now.

'When you went away, after the christening, Billy was too small to know you,' she assured him. 'Since I brought you home, he has seen you often, but never with your eyes open and never standing up. You frightened him because he does not understand the change.'

'Neither do I,' Will said softly, almost to himself. Then he added, 'He has no reason to fear.' He turned to look at her, as though to reassure her as well. 'I am not such a great beast, once you get to know me.'

She fought back her fears and laid a hand on his arm. 'He will learn that, in time.'

He gave the barest of nods. 'I hope you learn the same. I have not treated you very well, since I have awakened. But everything is so strange.' He turned back to the mirror, staring into it as though he expected to see something in her reversed reflection that was not apparent when he looked directly at her.

She resisted the urge to search her own face in the glass. How should one look, at a moment like this? She had learned for most of her adult life to be good at dissembling. But was anyone this good of an actress, to pull off such a stunning performance for an audience of one who would be watching her closely, searching for clues that might lead him to his own truth?

For her sister's sake, she had no choice but to try. She gave him a hopeful, watery smile and managed a single tear to indicate that her heart was too full for words. It gave her a few more moments to compose her thoughts before speaking. 'I do not fear you,' she lied. 'And I understand that it will take time before you can feel truly yourself again.'

'I am told my recovery thus far is thanks to your

care.' His brow was still furrowed as he repeated what must be rote acknowledgements of the situation as it had been told to him. 'But in truth, madam, I can remember nothing before yesterday, of you and our marriage. Please enlighten me. How did we come to be together?' His questions today lacked the accusatory tone of yesterday. He was not so much demanding answers, as honestly curious. It was as though he expected Scheherazade with a story so captivating he could not resist.

What could she tell him that would set his mind at rest? 'You arrived in Bath, after the crocuses were finished blooming, in May,' she said, trying to focus on a happy memory.

'In what month did we marry?'

'June,' she replied. It was a fine month for weddings, real or imaginary.

'Adam said we married in Gretna.' He said this almost to himself, as though calculating miles between the points.

'But we met in Bath,' she repeated, searching for a likely story. 'We met in a shop.' It was true. But she could not exactly tell him it was Montague and de Bryun, Purveyors of Fine Jewellery. 'I taught needlework, in a school for young girls. I wished to sell some of the handiworks there.' Hadn't that been her dream, at one time? To make a modest living with her hands.

'What was I doing in a lady's haberdashery?' he said, obviously surprised.

'You followed me there, I think,' she said, smiling at her own carelessness for choosing such an outlandish meeting place. 'I saw you enter the shop and everything changed.' That was very true. But it had not been for the better.

'You were taken with me?' Apparently, his ego had not been damaged, for she saw the slight swell of pride.

'You are a most handsome man.' Again, it was truth. She remembered the little thrill of excitement she'd felt, at seeing such a dashing man enter the salon. It was followed by the crashing realisation that he was a Felkirk.

'And what did I think of you?'

That had been obvious as well. She had introduced Mr Montague as her employer. But William Felkirk had seen the low-cut satin gowns she wore and the possessive way Montague treated her and known that her duties for the man were not limited to modelling the wares they sold. Then his lip had curled, ever so slightly, with contempt. 'I think you felt sorry for me,' she said, wishing it were true.

'So I offered to rescue you from your dreary life?' He raised an eyebrow.

'I refused you at first,' she embroidered. If she was to create a fairy-tale romance, there should be details. 'I did not think your offer was quite proper.'

'But I won you over with my charm and sincerity,' he said with such obvious doubt that it made her laugh.

'You took me on walks around the Crescent. We

met again in the assembly rooms and tea shops. You made it clear to me that your intentions were honourable.' Hadn't she envied many young couples, courting in just such a way on the other side of the shop window? Sometimes she saw them later, in the showroom, admiring the rings. 'When you made your offer, of course I accepted.'

'Of course,' he said dubiously. 'But what was I doing in Bath? I loathe the place.'

This was a wrinkle she had not accounted for. 'What were you doing in Bath? You did not say. What do most people do there? Take the waters. Attend parties.'

'I have managed to resist such activities thus far,' he said sceptically. 'Why would I decide to do them now?'

'I really have no idea. You did remark that you were bored,' she allowed. 'But that you liked it better, once you had met me.'

'And then we eloped.' He must suspect that this was unlikely. Having met his family and seen how close he was to them, she was sure, when he found the perfect wife, he would bring her to them, immediately.

'You were unwilling to wait, even for the reading of the banns, or the time to procure a special licence. And I was...' She took a deep breath and plunged forward with the biggest lie of all. 'Your affections were very difficult to resist. Impossible, in fact. Afterwards, you deemed it best that we marry with all haste and inform the family afterwards.'

'I see.' Now he was the one who was blushing. Let him think he had taken advantage and owed her some reparation. It would be true, soon enough. He was staring at her reflection in the mirror again. 'I do not doubt that I was insistent, once I set my cap for you. You are quite the prettiest woman I have ever seen.'

'Thank you.' She had grown used to accepting the words as a compliment, though they sometimes felt more like a curse. How different might her life have been had she been plain and undesirable? She might have gone unnoticed through life and kept her virtue. She certainly would not be in a ducal manor, flirting with a peer's brother. 'I was honoured by your attentions. I am sure there were others more appropriate for the brother of a duke, than an *émigrée* without family or fortune.'

He touched a finger to her lips. 'Do not speak so about yourself. You have proven more than worthy, since the accident.' The moment of spontaneous intimacy shocked them both and he carefully removed his hand.

'Thank you,' she said, wishing she could take the compliment as it was.

'But the accident,' he added. 'Tell me about it.'

She gave an honest shudder at the memory of him lying broken on the floor. Then she lied again. 'You were trying to impress me. A jump went wrong.'

'But what of Jupiter?'

For a moment, she was completely puzzled. Was this some obsession with astronomy that she had not known? Perhaps he was the sort who thought his life was ruled by the stars. Then she realised that he was referring to the horse. What had become of the horse? She had no idea. If Montague was aware of it, he had surely sold it by now. Or perhaps it was still in a stable in Bath, waiting for its owner to return. 'I am sorry, but his leg was broken. There was nothing that could be done...' It was kinder that he think the animal dead, than to realise that no one had cared enough to find it.

He held up a hand and turned his face away from hers, as though unwilling to let her finish. The weight of his body sagged against his crutches, as if he could not support himself. When she reached out to steady him, and to offer comfort, she felt the shuddering sob even as he shrugged off her touch.

In a moment, he straightened and composed himself. 'Then I deserved what I got,' he said, in a voice full of self-disgust. 'Taking foolish risks and putting another life in jeopardy. What the devil was I thinking to harm an animal that had been a faithful friend to me for seven years?'

If she had hoped to comfort him, she had failed completely. Felkirk was even more upset than he had been when leaving the parlour. And he grieved for a horse? When she'd met him, she had assumed that he and his family cared for nothing but their money and themselves. They certainly had not cared for her father, as he'd lain dying on their property so long ago.

But the duke and Penny had not been as she'd expected and had treated her as a long-lost sister. Now, the man in front of her was practically undone over the death of a beast. She wanted to take back the words and assure him that, somewhere, the horse was alive and well. Fine blood stock, like Jupiter probably was, would not have sold for hide and hoof to pay a stable bill.

Instead, she remained silent and let him lean upon her, as he struggled to regain his composure. 'Do you wish me to call for Stewart?' she said softly.

He shook his head, once, emphatically. Then he pulled himself upright and took a deep breath. 'This is too embarrassing. But so much of my life is, it seems.'

'It is not your fault,' she assured him. 'And I have seen you worse. Let me help you back to your room.'

He gave a very weak laugh as they made their way to the stairs. 'That does nothing to console me. The last thing a man wants to be is helpless in the presence of a beautiful woman.' He stopped for a moment and wiped a hand across his face. 'And weeping over a horse. You must think me mad as well as crippled.'

'The physicians did say you might not be yourself,' she reminded him.

He gave her another wry smile. 'It does not reassure me to hear I might run mad and no one will think twice about it. I am sorry to inform you of this, my dear. But I cannot blame a head injury on my tears over the loss of old Jupe. He was a fine horse and my truest friend. I must have told you how long we were together.'

'I understand,' she said, trying not to appear relieved. His upset, no matter how unjustified, had been a help. He was too busy trying to save some scrap of dignity to ask any more questions of her.

He paused, took a firm grip on the stair rail and gave another quick wipe of his eyes with the back of his hand before moving up another step. 'All the same, I apologise. If I am still not the master of body or mind, I am unfit company. It was a mistake to inflict myself on others this evening.'

'You cannot be expected to hide in your room for ever. And you are doing much better than yesterday,' she added, since it was perfectly true. Now that he was awake, the speed of his recovery was impressive. 'The family is eager to see you and will be patient.'

'Not too patient,' he said, wiping the last moisture from his eyes. 'I am barely on my feet again and Adam means to put us out.'

'No.' She had no right to think it. Had she forgotten she was an interloper here? This was not her home and she must not think of it as such. But if she did not live here, then where was she to go?

Felkirk gave her a wan smile. 'I said something similar, when he suggested it. But he is right. I have a home of my own, less than a mile from here.' He paused, then said, 'We have a home. It is where we belong. Tomorrow, you shall see.'

'But…' What was she to tell Montague? And how was she to tell him? There was no time to leave a signal.

They had reached the top of the stairs and Felkirk balanced carefully on a single crutch and draped his free arm about her shoulders. 'You have nothing to worry about. Adam was right to suggest it, as you were just now. I cannot hide in my room for ever, assuming I will improve. And we cannot use the size of this place, and the presence of Adam and Penny, to hide from each other.'

Had it been so obvious that she was avoiding him? She could not think of an answer to it, so busied herself with helping him the last few feet down the hall to his room. They were standing outside the door to his sickroom. The valet was no doubt waiting inside to help him to bed. If he did not need her any longer, she could make her excuses and escape to the ground floor to tell the family that he had retired. He might be sound asleep by the time she returned. He was right that she could not avoid him for ever. But was one more night so much to ask?

She dropped her gaze to the floor and offered a curtsy. It was probably not the way a loving wife was supposed to behave. She should be warmer, bolder and unafraid to catch his eye. But when he was near like this, she could not think clearly. What was to become of her, once they were out of this house and had only each other for company? She turned away, glancing back down the hall. 'If you do not need me any longer, I will return to the parlour and explain to the family.'

'There is one last thing,' he said, as though something had just occurred to him and gestured her close again, as though about to whisper.

She leaned in as well.

Then he kissed her. It was just a buss upon the lips. It was so quick and sweet that she gasped in surprise. And for a moment, her mind was calm. Not empty, as it was when she was with Montague. It was as placid as a lake on a windless day. Then she felt the faintest ripples of expectation. Was she actually hoping for another kiss?

'Thank you, for your help. And your devotion,' he said. There was no indication of his feelings on the matter, other than the faintest of smiles.

'It was...' Why could she not find her words? And why could she not draw away from him? She was leaning against him, as though she was the one who needed crutches. Montague would not have approved. He had sent her here as a seductress. He did not want her behaving like some moonstruck girl...

The second kiss that she had been hoping for came in a rush of sweetness, soft as the wing of a moth. William Felkirk braced himself against the doorframe of his room and pulled her body to him, letting the wall support them both. Then he touched his lips to hers and moved them slowly, tenderly, before closing them once, twice, three times, against her mouth.

Why did she feel so breathless? Montague would have laughed and called her a fool. But she did not want to think of him, just now. Instead, she focused on the slight cleft in the chin that hovered before her eyes as those same gentle lips kissed her forehead. There was a faint shadow there, where his valet had missed a whisker or two. She wanted to kiss him there, to trace the crease with her tongue and feel the roughness of the stubble.

She had waited too long. Felkirk was setting her back on her feet, smiling down into her face. And for the first time, she saw the easy smile and friendly nature his family assured her was his by habit. 'You are right, my dear. You must go back to the parlour. And I must rest. Much as I would like to say otherwise, I fear there are things I am simply not yet capable of.'

He meant bed play. She did not know if it was proper for a wife to do so, but she blushed at the thought.

It made him laugh. 'Although, with you here, looking as you do, I will pray most fervently for a return to health and strength.'

'I will pray for you, as well,' she agreed.

'And pray for my memory,' he added. 'I cannot recall what we have meant to each other. But I am sure, once you are in my arms, it will all come back to me.'

She thought of the beads she kept in her dresser. She would tell them tonight, several times over, and hope that the quantity of prayer for a selective memory might counter anything he had asked for.

Chapter Seven

Now that William Felkirk was awake, Justine was discovering the inconveniences of married life. When he had been in a coma, there had been little question as to who made the decisions. On the rare occasions she had been overruled by the duke as to the best method to tend the invalid, it had been the result of discussion and not flat mandate. But now that he was awake, Lord Felkirk expected not just an equal share in his recovery, but the deciding vote in all matters.

After the discussion in the hall, she had hoped that there would be some time to persuade him of the need for caution before a change of location. But when she awakened the next morning, the arrangements for the move back to his own home were already in progress and would be done before noon. The valet seemed relieved to be packing up the limited supply of garments and his lord's shaving kit. Her own garments were only slightly more troublesome, for she had brought a single trunk with her, when she'd come north. Penny offered her the use of the maid she'd had, until she was able to choose someone from her own household. The girl had already gone ahead and was probably already hanging gowns and pressing ribbons in their new home.

In the midst of the activity, William Felkirk paced the floor as though he could not wait to be under way. Though he had claimed to be reticent, he had obviously warmed to his brother's advice and meant to act on it immediately. 'It makes no sense to maintain a second household, less than a mile from the first,' he said. 'It is unfair to expect servants to fetch and carry items between the two. I have a perfectly good home, just down the road from here. I mean to live in it.'

'But you are still so weak,' she said. She cast a sidelong glance at the crutches in the corner and wondered if their kiss in the hallway had given him this burst of energy.

'It is not as if I intend to walk the distance,' he informed her. 'A carriage ride will be no more strenuous than sitting in a Bath chair. The air of the journey will likely do me good.'

'The doctor—' she said plaintively.

'—lives closer to the old manor than he does to this one. And do not tell me that the stairs will be unfamiliar, or the rooms inconvenient. It is the home I grew up in and I know each step of it. It is also a damned sight smaller than this cavernous place of my brother's. It feels like I must walk a mile here, just to get from bed to breakfast.'

His words stopped her objections. 'You did not always live here, in the duke's manor?'

'Heavens, no.' William shook his head and smiled. 'Mother did not like the old house at all. It had been fine for ten generations of Bellstons, but she wanted a ballroom and a grand dining hall. It is good that she did not live to see Adam nearly burn the place to the ground a few years ago. She would have been appalled. But that is another story.'

'How long ago was that?' she asked, trying to suppress her excitement.

'The fire?' he asked.

'No. The building of the new manor.'

'A little less than fifteen years,' he said, taking a moment to count on his fingers. 'In the end, it was a sensible decision. I am able to stay on the family lands without living in my brother's pocket. The two manors are close enough to share the stables, the ice house and the gardens.' He grinned. 'I have all the advantages of being a duke and none of the responsibilities.'

Fifteen years. Her father had been dead for twenty. If there were clues to be had about the murder or the missing diamonds, she had been searching the wrong house for them. Surely they must be at the old manor, the place where she would soon be living.

'I think you are probably right, then,' she said, trying not to sound too excited. 'A change will do you good.' And it would give her an opportunity to search the rooms there that she had not already seen. When she found a way to get the information to him, Montague would be pacified. It would give her time to think of a next step that might keep Margot safe from his threats.

It also meant that she would be alone with her husband. There would be no duke and duchess to fill the days and evenings spent in company with him. The odds increased that his memory might return, or she would let slip some bit of the truth that could not be easily distracted by turning it to another subject.

But when darkness fell, there would be no reason for them to talk at all. As she had on the previous evening, she felt a strange anticipation, like the stillness in the air before a storm.

'You will like it,' he said, mistaking her silence for more understandable worries. 'Just wait. You shall be mistress over your own home. In no time at all, you will have arranged everything to suit yourself and we shall return Adam and Penny's hospitality.'

Her own household. What a strange idea. While she had experience in managing servants for Mr Montague, she had seen the way they looked at her, half in pity and half in disapproval, as though it pained them to take their instructions from the master's whore. Now she was to be the lady of a manor and no one would doubt that it was her proper place. If the situation weren't so dire, she might have been excited at the thought.

Once they were underway, it appeared that William was right about his need to make the move. As she sat in his side in the carriage, she could see his mood lightening with each turn of the wheels. He stared out the window so intently that she almost thought he was avoiding her gaze. At last, he said, 'It is good to be coming home again. There is much about the current situation that is strange to me. Having to deal with it in my brother's house made it no easier.'

'They have been very kind to me, during our stay there,' she remarked.

'I would expect nothing less of them,' he said. 'But when we married, I am sure it was not our intent to live out the remainder of our lives in someone else's house.'

'True,' she agreed.

'We are barely out of our honeymoon, are we not?' It was a perfectly innocent remark and a logical reason to wish to be alone together. But they both fell silent at the thought.

'We have not known each other long,' she answered. 'And it has been a very unusual few months.'

They both fell silent again.

He took a breath and began again. 'I will be frank with you, since it makes no sense not to be. I do not know you, as a husband should.'

'Your accident…' she said, searching for a way to explain the perfectly logical absence of romantic memories.

'Is in the past,' he finished for her. 'I do not remember you. But if we are to be married, it does no good for me to be dwelling on that fact. I… We…' he amended. 'We must move forward with what is left. And it will be impossible if we continue to avoid each other, relying on family and friends to fill the gaps and sleeping on opposite sides of a closed door.' Then he exhaled, as if it had taken an effort to state the obvious.

'It was you who sent me away,' she reminded him, careful to keep the censure from her voice. If they had truly been married she likely would have been hurt and angered by his rejection. But the sensible reaction was the one most likely to reveal her lies.

'I was wrong to do so,' he replied. 'If we are married…'

'If?' she countered.

'Now that we are married,' he corrected, 'we must accept the fact that the last six months change nothing. I have spoken to my brother and I do not think an annulment is possible.'

How could one dissolve a marriage that did not exist in the first place? She ignored the real question and chose another. 'Did you wish to cast me off, then?'

She could see the change in his face, as he realised how cruel his words had been. When he spoke again, it was after some thought. 'If I did, it was unfair of me, just as it was when I sent you from my bedroom. When we arrive at the house, I will instruct the servants to place your things in the room beside mine, for the sake of convenience. But from this point forward, I expect you to share my bed.'

'As you wish, my lord.' When Montague had informed her of her future, he had done it with a similar lack of passion. She had been foolish to imagine, after a kiss or two, it would be any different with this man.

Beside her, Lord Felkirk swore under his breath. 'I did not mean it to sound like a command.'

'You are my husband,' she said, with as much confidence as she could manage. 'I have promised to obey. It shall be just as you wish and I will do my best to give you no reason to be unhappy.'

Apparently, she had failed in that already. He was frowning. Despite his earlier excitement, he looked no happier when they reached the house. 'My home,' Will said in a tired voice, and waited for her comment.

She was not sure what she had expected, but it had not been this. It was not the thoroughly modern manor that the duke inhabited, with its large windows and perfectly matched wings. The old manor still held traces of the fortress it had once been. On the left, a square tower ended in wide crenellations. There was nothing left of the right tower but a low wall of grey stone to mark the edge of the kitchen garden. Though a Gothic stone arch remained around the iron-bound front door, the rest of the main building had been rebuilt of brick by some misguided architect of another century.

It was a hodge-podge of styles and Justine could see why the previous duchess had been eager to build a new manor. She understood, but she could not agree. 'You live in a castle,' she announced, then scolded herself for stating the obvious.

'Part of one,' he said. 'There is not much of the old building left.'

'It does not matter.' She stared up at the tower in front of them. 'It is magnificent.'

'You like it?' He seemed surprised at her enthusiasm.

'You do not?' She stared back at him, equally surprised.

'Well, yes, actually. I do. But I grew up here. Perhaps that is why I am willing to overlook its obvious flaws.'

She stared back at the old manor and could not help smiling at its lopsided grandeur. 'Well, I see no problems with it. It has character,' she said, wondering why he could not see it.

'As you wish,' he said, giving a dismissive nod of his head and turning away from her again. The servants had lined up at the door, eager to greet the master on his homecoming and to officially welcome the lady of the house. William walked unsteadily before her, smiling more warmly at the butler than he ever had at her, and accepting the arm of a footman to help him up the last steps and into his home.

Though he had claimed the trip would be an easy one, it was clear that the activity had tired him. 'I think, if you have no need of me, that I shall retire to my room for a time.'

'You must do as you see fit,' she said. 'We will have more than enough time to talk, now that we are home.' The word stuck in her throat, but she forced it out.

He nodded and muttered something to the footman at his side, who took his arm and helped him to climb the stairs to his room.

Which left Justine alone with the servants and the house. She gave a sigh of relief at being free of him, if only for an hour or two. Then she gave instructions for the unpacking of their things and discussed the luncheon menu with the housekeeper. Then she enquired, oh so casually, about the best room to find pen, ink and paper. She wished to write to tell a friend of her move.

The housekeeper, Mrs Bell, directed her to the morning room without further enquiry and left her to pen a hurried note to Mr Smith, the *nom de guerre* that Montague had chosen for his stay at a nearby inn.

She imagined the way it would travel to him, on the road to the village, which lay equidistant between the two manors. Her father had travelled that road, on the night he died. At the turning, he had gone left and not right, as she'd assumed. She had thought, on her morning walks, that she had been retracing his last footsteps, but she had not gone far enough.

His goal had been this house. His death had been on these grounds. Any clue to the murder, or the missing jewels, would be under this very roof.

She had but to find it and then the jewels. Then, she would rescue Margot and they would run away, all without revealing the truth to either William Felkirk or John Montague.

When put that way, it was hard to be optimistic.

Chapter Eight

Justine was already seated at the luncheon table when Will came down from his nap. He found it faintly annoying. He was unaccustomed to seeing anyone across the table from him, much less a person who would arrive before he had so that she might be ready to attend him. Here she was, fresh, cheerful and inescapable in a muslin gown and starched cap, offering to prepare his plate or help him in any way she could.

He did not want help. He wanted to be left alone to understand what had happened to him. It was an urge he must learn to ignore. After his brave words in the coach about facing troubles and moving forward, he had taken the first opportunity to escape to his room for a sulk.

At least, now that he was free of his brother's home, he would not have to see the ring of happy faces about him, convinced that everything was fine when he was sure it was not. There was only one face before him now. Though it was beautiful, it had the same detached expression it had worn since the first. If they were truly so alike as Adam thought, she should be as angry with him as he was with himself. He had ordered her to bed as though her wants and needs meant nothing at all. She had responded as though she had no feelings to hurt.

Perhaps she was waiting for the same thing he was: a sudden rush of memory that would explain all. But it seemed she viewed it with the strange dread he did. 'Are you not going to ask me if I have remembered anything, now that I am home?' he said, watching her intently as she poured the wine.

She took a sip from her glass. 'I expect, if you do remember anything, I will be the first to know. You do not mean to hide the truth from me, do you?' Her eyes were wide and innocent as though the idea that he might not share all his thoughts had never occurred to her.

It made him feel like a cad for barking at her. 'Of course not,' he said hurriedly. What reason would he have to conceal what he knew? After his talk of annulment, she must think he meant to negate their marriage by feigning ignorance of it. Even if he did not wish for a wife, he would not abandon this one to her ruin, just to avoid a forgotten bad decision.

He spoke again, in a gentler tone. 'It is good to be home. I found the attention at Adam's house to be rather oppressive.'

'It is because they care for you,' she said. 'They

cannot help but crowd you. Would you not have done the same for your brother, in a similar situation?'

He thought back for a moment. 'I suspect I already have. There was a time, a few years back, where Adam had difficulties. I suppose I've told you that the scars on my arm came from a fire that he caused?'

She seemed to consider for a moment, then nodded as though his statement had answered an unasked question.

Surely he had explained the damaged patch of skin to her on their first night together. She must have noticed it. The smooth red mark stretching from elbow to shoulder was impossible to miss. He was self-conscious about it and quick to offer explanation, so as not to alarm the women he took to his bed. But his own wife was looking at him as though he had said not a word to her on the subject. It was strange.

But it was just one of many strange things that had happened in the last week. He willed himself to forget it, and began again, cautiously. 'I wanted to help Adam then and was told on several occasions to go to the Devil. I questioned his wisdom in marrying Penny as well.'

'You disapproved?' Now Justine's eyes were round with surprise.

'I was wrong, of course. But that did not stop me from speaking. Tim Colton went through his own dark time, after his first wife died. He is a particular friend of Adam's, so I did not have to bear the brunt of his moods. But apparently his behaviour was extreme. He also refused the help of his friends.'

'So you are telling me that all men are difficult?' Justine said, with a slight arch of her eyebrow.

'All men around here, at any rate. Perhaps it is the climate in Wales that leads us to be melancholy and pigheaded.'

She nodded. 'Then if you snap and grumble, I shall not blame myself for it.'

'You needn't. It is my problem, not yours,' he said. He thought back to his suspicions of the previous day and wondered if that was true. If she was the one keeping secrets, he would be quite justified in blaming her. But to look at her now, fresh and pretty in the afternoon sunlight, it seemed churlish to find fault with her.

He took a bit of cold salmon and a swallow of wine, and admired her over the rim of his wine glass.

She was nibbling on a bit of roll and glanced up to catch him staring at her. She put it down and spoke. 'Now that you are home, what are your plans? I assume that I am not oppressing you by enquiring.' There was the faintest twitch at the corner of her mouth and he wondered if she meant to be amusing.

It was rather amusing to think of her attention as a heavy burden. She seemed to work at being unobtrusive. Beautiful to look at, but quiet as a ghost, she hovered barely noticed on the fringe of any conversation. When he needed her, she came just close enough to help, then disappeared again, like a sprite.

Perhaps that was why he had married her. To find a woman willing to fit herself seamlessly into his life was a rare piece of good fortune.

She was enquiring after his plans. What were they? Many of the activities he might have favoured were quite beyond him, until he regained his strength. 'I don't have any,' he admitted.

'Then might I trouble you to show me around your home?' she said. 'The housekeeper will do it, if you do not wish to. But I suspect it would be more interesting to hear the details of the place from you. It is many hours before you mean to bed me. We must find some way to pass the afternoon.'

He choked on his next swallow of wine. When he could compose himself to look at her again, there was no sign that she had been laughing. But he was quite sure she had been. It was a promising sign.

He would enjoy walking the halls of his own home, again. And to show it to one of the few women in England who seemed to appreciate its design. Even Penny, who had few strong opinions about anything outside of her books had proclaimed the place an eyesore and suggested that he tear it down and rebuild from the foundation up.

Perhaps Adam had been right all along and he had simply married a woman who suited his character. It would be interesting to see if her opinions matched his on the interior. For though the decoration was not the current style, he liked it very well. He might regain some of his strength as they walked from room to room and pause to rest as needed, under the guise of telling her old family stories.

And why did he suspect that she knew just that and had found a perfect way to preserve his dignity while encouraging him to exercise his wasted legs? 'A tour sounds like an excellent idea,' he agreed. 'Let us finish our meal and we can begin.' Perhaps if he spent the day with her, he would learn something of her as well.

But, after an afternoon of walking the house, he knew no more about her than when they began. She was an attentive audience and he took pleasure in regaling her with childhood tales about growing up in the old manor. But she offered no similar details of her own youth. It was nearly time to dress for supper and the sum total of his knowledge was no greater than when they had begun. She was beautiful. She was Belgian. She was an orphan. She had impeccable manners and made lace, though he had never seen her wear any. And she was most grateful to be married to him and eager to see to his comfort in all things.

As they walked, she seemed to sense when he was tiring and took his arm, as though she was too shy to walk alone. When she suspected that they had gone too long without a break, she claimed exhaustion and requested they sit for a time, in the conservatory, or the music room, which she had guessed were his favourites. In all things she supported him, while persuading him that he was, in fact, supporting her.

She was the perfect wife.

Or nearly perfect. Should it be so disquieting to have such a devoted helpmeet? He could not find fault with her looks. She was quite the loveliest woman he could imagine. But it was as if a painting had come to life, or a statue. There was no passion in her. Her red-gold hair was contained beneath a cloth cap. Her shapely body hid beneath a modest gown. At the table, she had shocked him with her frank acceptance of tonight's possible activities. But once they were in bed, would she be an enthusiastic lover? Or would she be as mild as she was here in the drawing room, listening intently as he described the family members in the portraits and the history of each ornament on the shelves? Did she truly have no character other than the one she assumed he wished to see?

He was sure his married brother could explain to him the dangers of a wife who wished to be contrary. But to have found one that was nothing more than a mirror reflection of his own opinions was not as pleasant as it sounded.

They had walked nearly back to the bedrooms, now, and were standing in front of the nursery. He paused, strangely unwilling to open the door. 'We needn't bother with this,' he said, stepping back from it. 'There is nothing within but old playthings. But you will find the rooms to be most sensible, when we need them for our children.'

'Of course,' she said. And just as strangely, she stepped away as well.

'Now that Adam has started his family, we can be reasonably sure of the succession,' he remarked. 'The need for a son is not pressing.'

'We needn't rush,' she agreed. 'Unless, that is what you wish,' she added hurriedly. Once again, there was the slight, acquiescent bow of the head, as though she would try to produce an entire family for him, right now, should that be his desire.

As if he wished to raise children with a stranger. Despite her looks, he was not even sure he truly wanted to bed her. There would be no joy in it if her response was apathetic acceptance of the act. What was the point of marrying a beautiful woman, if one had to find an equally pretty mistress who would at least feign enthusiasm for his lovemaking?

Then he looked forward, into the nursery again, remembered the reason for wives and retreated. 'We will discuss such matters again when I am fully recovered.'

'Of course,' she agreed, turning away to return to her room.

Justine did her best to maintain her composure in the hours that followed, but her new husband made it more challenging than she'd expected. When she'd first hit upon this scheme, she had not thought that such an evening was in her future. Though she would do her best to save him, William Felkirk was going to die.

She had been sure of it. She'd felt terror mixed with pity at the sight of his bleeding head and Mr

Montague's dispassionate expression as he raised the poker for a second blow. Before he could strike, she'd hurried to convince him that the man would be better off in the bosom of his family than as a corpse on the floor of their salon. What would happen if the Duke of Bellston appeared in Bath, enquiring after his missing brother?

Worse yet, suppose he sent the law? There was no question that they would both hang for murder. Margot would be left alone, with nothing but the scandalously false broadsheet confession of Montague's mistress: the salacious details of a good woman brought low by her own depravity.

She had insisted that further violence against William Felkirk was unnecessary. If the blow did not kill him, the trip north likely would. If he survived that? Then she would linger for a time, until she had discovered the diamonds and could disappear.

But now he was across the dinner table from her, eager to rebuild his imagined past. Escape was impossible, if he meant to watch her every bite. What would he expect of her, now that they would have so many hours together? The tour of the house had been helpful and she had seen a half-score of rooms where she might search for information about her father.

But they could not spend each day in rambling about the house together. Nor would he wish to spend his evenings thus. Along with the letter to Montague, she had scribbled a hurried note to Penny and begged her to come to dinner, hoping to alleviate this awkward togetherness.

The duchess had sent an equally hurried response. 'You need time to get to know one another again,' she had said. 'You do not need the distraction of others. In a week, perhaps, we shall come to see how you are getting on.'

A week? Penny might as well have said a year, for all the help that offered. Justine had sighed and informed the housekeeper that all meals would be served 'for two.' And that was a problem in itself. She had no idea what her husband's favourite foods were, his schedule when home, or even what rooms he took his meals in. She would have to rely on the servants. With the instruction, she had added a shy flutter of her lashes and a worried look. Then she had remarked that he had been sick for so long she'd feared ever having this opportunity...

The housekeeper had rushed to her aid, promising that every effort would be made to help her learn the likes and dislikes of the master, and the proper running of the house. The woman's eagerness to help her made her feel like even more of a liar than usual.

But trusting Mrs Bell had led to the table in the main dining room, facing an excess of silver and crystal, and a banquet clearly meant as a triumphant celebration of their return home. The man who could barely lift his fork two days before was enjoying nine courses and three wines.

Though he ate with obvious relish, she could feel

his eyes upon her, just as Montague's were, when they were alone together. His gaze was possessive, as though he was admiring some lovely ornament on a shelf, still surprised that he had come to own it. Soon, he would take it down and run his hands over it, to learn its every contour and detail. She shivered again.

He glanced immediately to the far side of the room, to the unlit fireplace. 'You will find that old houses such as this are draughty. It is as if the chill settles into the stone, even in summer. Shall I call for a servant to light a fire?'

'It is not necessary,' she assured him. 'We will not be here for long. If it bothers me again, I will remember to bring a shawl to dinner.'

'Oh.' There was a faint downward inflection, as though the idea that she might hide her bare shoulders disappointed him. Why did he not simply refuse her the comfort? She had long ago learned not to make such requests of Montague, for fear that he would insist she must wear even less, to show her obedience. When one had been given the choice of just a gown, or just a shawl, one learned to ignore the cold.

Now, Lord Felkirk pushed his dessert away. 'There is no need for an ice so late in the season, no matter how beautifully it is presented.' He stared down at the china ice-cream pot on the table, its lid heaped with ice to keep the contents cool. The butter, as well, rested in a basin of ice so that it might keep its perfect mould of the Felkirk family crest. He stared at the display and shook his head. 'So cold, all of it. Cold as the grave.'

As Justine watched, his attention slipped from her. He had gone oddly pensive, of a sudden, his expression darkening as though his mind wandered in a cavern somewhere, further and further from the light of day. It was almost as unsettling as his earlier thoughts. 'Let us retire to the salon,' she suggested. 'There is a fire laid there. I am sure it will be most cosy.' She feared that was rather an overstatement of the truth. Although the old manor was smaller than the new one, it was still too large to house a single couple. At the very least, it should hold two rambunctious boys, as it had in William's youth.

But the man before her was no longer an energetic child. When he stood, he offered his arm. But they both knew that what appeared an ordinary courtesy was a subtle request for her support so that he might manage with just a walking stick and not crutches. As she had in the afternoon, she came to his side and they proceeded together down the hall.

In the formal sitting room, she led him to a divan and poured him his port. Then she took her own place in a chair opposite, where her lacemaking pillow had been arranged for her. The evening was likely to be a silent affair, as full of thoughtful glances and mutual speculation as dinner had been. They were strangers, after all. There was little they had to converse about.

Necessary though it was, she could not bring herself to create any more memories out of whole cloth, demanding that he believe anecdotes from their courtship and elopement. There was only one thing she wished to discuss and the topic was unreachable. What was it about his house that had set him looking for a diamond pouch that had been missing and forgotten since late in the last century?

She made a covert study of the room: fireplace and mantel, landscapes on the wall, rug thick, but flat. There were no obvious hiding places here. She could not imagine herself stomping about the place, sounding for loose floorboards and hollow compartments. As her husband stood and approached her, she could not help but listen, hoping that one of his steps might sound different from another, revealing a trapdoor in the planking. But each sounded the same as the other, until he stopped just short of her, staring down as she worked.

She paused and looked up, expecting to see the censure she received from Montague when she occupied herself with something other than his needs. 'If you wish, you have but to say the word and I will put it away.'

'No. No, certainly not.' He took a step back as though surprised at her response. 'If it gives you pleasure, by all means continue.'

She offered a nod of thanks. Though she had not given it much thought, it did give her pleasure. While her hands were busy, her mind was free as a bird to think whatever she liked.

She felt him shift uncomfortably, foot to foot, and wondered if he wished for a similar pursuit. Perhaps he was as unsure of his place in this new world as she was. She raised her eyes from the mechanical motion of her hands on the bobbins and said, 'What do you normally do, of an evening, to pass the time?'

'You do not know?' he asked, almost suspiciously.

Her mind raced for a moment, then settled on an answer. 'We were together only a short while. You had little time or interest in domestic pleasures. In fact, I did not pick up my lace again until after we arrived in Wales and I knew you were settled comfortably. There simply was not time for it.' She waited for him to infer the obvious.

'We spent more time in the bedroom than the drawing room?' he said, then laughed at her blush. 'It need not embarrass you. We are married and our behaviour was quite normal.'

'Of course,' she responded. Now that she had put the thought into his head, he would likely demand that they retire immediately to return to their old diversions. At least the suspense would end and she could settle her nerves. Lying on one's back in silence was easier by far than trying to think of what to say while sitting up.

He looked at her thoughtfully for a moment, then said, 'I am sure, with practice, we can learn to sit together in the parlour as well. You asked how I spend my evenings when at home?' He paused again. 'I like to read. Not very exciting, I suppose. You may have noticed that my brother is happiest pacing about the room and debating politics. And while Penny is a great reader, she is often translating from Greek or Latin as she does so.' He paused, as though it were some sort of guilty secret. 'But I prefer novels.'

'Do you read aloud?' she asked. It was a solution that would solve no end of trouble. He might be happy and conversation would be rendered impossible.

He thought for a moment. 'I have not done it thus far. Until recently, I have not had an audience.'

'I should be happy to listen,' she said, 'if you wish to do so.'

'It would not distract you?'

'It would be a welcome addition to the evening,' she assured him. 'Perhaps you could choose one of your favourites, to share with me.'

He had responded to this with a relieved smile that made her wonder if the ensuing hours weighed as heavily on him as they did on her. When he had taken up his cane to go to the library for a book, he had waved away her offer of help. Both his spirit and his step had seemed lighter.

The answering warm glow she felt inside on seeing the change surprised her. Perhaps she had grown so used to thinking of him as her patient that she took credit for his success. Or maybe it was the equally unexpected knowledge that she did not like seeing him unhappy. Before he had come into the shop in Bath, she had felt only bitterness at the thought of him and his family. But the man before her now was what her father might have described as *tabula rasa*: a blank slate on which anything might be written. It did not seem fair to hold the past against him.

When he returned from his search, he was barely winded by the trip down the hall and holding a battered copy of *Gulliver's Travels*. She could barely remember the story, but she was sure she had read it some time in childhood. But it was plain that she had not understood the finer points of the narrative. The passages, though very funny, were too bawdy to be read aloud in a drawing room. She did not know whether to laugh or blush, doing both by turns. What must he think of her?

Then she remembered that she was supposed to be his wife and should not be shocked by his choice of subject. Perhaps he meant to relax her and put her in the mood for what was likely to follow, once they had retired to his room. It was strange. If he meant to flirt with her, he needn't have bothered. He had but to command and she would do whatever he wished.

Or he could give her another kiss. The memory of the kiss in the hallway of his brother's home was far more shocking than anything he was reading and left her so flustered that she confused her twists with her crosses on a whole row of bobbins and had to undo them and start again.

What was she to make of him? It would be a lie to say she did not like his company. She had not expected to enjoy this time alone, or to be so entertained by a thing that obviously gave him pleasure. It made her think longingly of the library. There were enough books in it for a lifetime of evenings just like this one.

She had enjoyed listening to him this morning as well. His stories of home and family had been so interesting that she had almost forgotten the reason she had wished to hear them. Her father's fate, and the location of the gems, had seemed unimportant compared to the history of a place that would never be a true home to her.

She suspected it was its master who fascinated her, not the house itself. She liked to look at him, with his pale skin, black hair and fine features. Even as he'd lain in the sickbed, she'd had more than a nurse's interest in the naked body concealed beneath the sheet. Though it was wasting from prolonged illness, she could imagine the vitality that had been there. As he read to her tonight, she could see the vigour she had assumed was there. His enthusiasm for the book filled the room. His voice was expressive, his whole body animated, so she could imagine the scenes playing out before her. She had been right to bring him home. What a waste it would have been for someone so alive to die violently, alone and unloved.

She let herself relax into the sound of his voice and the flicker of the candle behind the screen at her side, her fingers working methodically on the trim in her lap. When he shut the book with a snap, she was surprised to hear the clock strike eleven. She looked up at him and he returned her gaze with a surprised smile.

'I did not think it had got so late,' she said.

'Nor had I.' He yawned and stood, setting the book aside. 'I think, perhaps, it is time for us to retire. Let me escort you to your room. When you are ready for bed…' he paused, as though he was as nervous as she. 'Come into my room by the connecting door. You need not bother to knock. I will be waiting for you.'

'Of course,' she agreed.

Chapter Nine

She did as he suggested, letting the maid that had come with her from Penny's household dress her in her nightgown and comb and braid her hair. With each stroke of the brush she reminded herself that it was foolish to be so nervous. She was not some fainting virgin, unaware of what was about to occur. Her time with Montague had prepared her for any request Lord Felkirk might make.

William, she reminded herself. His family called him Will. So must she think of him, for she was his wife. If the stories she had told him were true, they had been intimate for some time. They would be so again. It was only natural.

She fought down the depression that the thought caused. It was bad enough to be the plaything of Montague. But to open herself to a stranger in the hope of gain? It was a dangerous precedent.

The best she could hope for was that this would be the last man to use her so. But it was a shame that it had to be this particular man. He was kind. He was funny. And he was most certainly handsome. At one time, it had been her dream to find such a man. More accurately, she had wanted to be found by him. If only he could have come five years ago, before it was too late…

She dismissed the maid and took one more glance in the mirror, watching her own eyes go blank as she put such foolish thoughts aside. Then she went to the door that connected their rooms and turned the knob.

He was already in bed, smiling at her as she closed the door behind her. He had propped himself up on the pillows, bare arms folded behind his head. The covers pooled in his lap, exposing his equally bare chest. She suspected he was naked beneath them. For a moment, she wanted nothing more than to turn and run.

Foolishness. She had seen a naked man before. She had seen this man naked. She'd been bathing him for weeks. There were no surprises here.

He unfolded his arms and held one out to her in welcome, patting the mattress at his side with the other. 'Come,' he said.

Without thinking, she went to him, as obedient as a trained dog. Her own lack of resistance disgusted her. Had Montague schooled the last of the spirit from her? She buried the thought deep, so that it did not show on her face. It would not do to go frowning to her husband's bed.

As she drew near, he threw back the blankets

so that she might climb in beside him. She glanced down at the bare flank it revealed and then back up into his face, then sat down on the mattress, swung her legs up beside his and let him settle the covers over them.

His arm wrapped around her, holding her easily to his side. 'Is this as strange to you as it is to me?'

Stranger than he could possibly imagine. She sought a comfortable place to rest her own arms, settling them gently against his chest. 'It has been some time,' she said, trying to sound sympathetic.

'You, at least, remember who I am,' he pointed out.

'Will it really matter so much, once the lights are out?' she asked.

She had said something wrong. He leaned away from her, clearly shocked. Of course it should matter. If the man one loved could not remember, it should hurt. If he had cared enough to marry her, he should at least pretend that she was not just another warm body in his bed.

He cleared his throat. 'If it were simply a matter of desire, perhaps it would not matter. We share something more, do we not?' This last came with a leading, hopeful tone, as though he was still longing to remember what it was that had brought them to marry.

She had no answer, other than 'yes.' Then she snuggled closer to him and eased a leg over his, hoping that the discussion might be over for the night.

He did not move away. But neither did he tumble her on to her back so that they could begin. Instead, his other hand reached out to her. It hovered over her breasts for a moment. Then he ran a finger along the neckline of her rather chaste nightrail. 'Did you make this for yourself?'

'Of course.'

'And the lace here. What is it called?'

She shrugged, for it was no great achievement. 'A simple picot edging.'

'Do you make it with the pins and the cushion?'

She shook her head, surprised that he would be asking about her work now, of all times. 'I use a shuttle. It is called tatting. Very easy. I can make enough for the whole gown in an evening.'

He looked down at her body again, seemingly more interested in the simple dress than the body beneath it. 'Is this indicative of your other nightwear?'

'I have several identical to this,' she admitted.

'It is very practical,' he said, politely.

She had a sudden memory of lying with Montague, wearing the sheer lawn he preferred. And then there were the nights he expected her to come to him wearing nothing at all. She could not help the sudden shudder of revulsion.

He lifted the blanket and bunched it around her shoulders. 'As I told you before, old houses are cold. But you may trust that I will keep you warm when we are together like this.' With two fingers, he plucked the nightcap from her head and dropped it on the floor beside the bed. Then he blew a warm breath against her ear.

This made her shiver as well. But it was accompanied by a sigh of delight that surprised her and drew a satisfied nod from him. Then he spoke again. 'I am curious. You take the time to make masterpieces for your friends. They could talk of nothing else but the cleverness of your work. When I did not see lace trimming on your gown during the day, or at dinner, I assumed I would see some tonight.' He glanced down at the cap on the floor and shook his head in disappointment. 'Why do you not wear the finer stuff yourself?'

She had a sudden memory of the chest her mother had kept. It was as big as a wardrobe, the outside inlaid with intricate tracings of sulphur, the inside smelling of beeswax and cloves. *You will have it some day*, she had said. *For your trousseau.*

How long had it been since she'd thought of it? After Montague had come to her, she'd realised that marriage was a lost dream. That had been the day that she'd set the items she'd already made aside, so that Margot might have them.

Her husband was waiting for an answer.

'It is nice to see others happy,' she said.

'I would like to see you happy as well,' he replied. 'You would be most attractive in a gown trimmed with the lace you were making tonight.' He drew a finger across her bodice, as if to indicate where it might go.

She shivered. 'It would not be very modest. You would see...' She stopped. She could imagine her nipples, poking through the lace.

'I know,' he said, with a smile, his hand pausing dangerously near to one of them.

'If you wish, I will remove the gown,' she said, squirming under the covers to draw up the hem.

He covered her hand with his to stop her. 'You misunderstand me.'

Perhaps she did not. 'You do not wish to see my body?'

He gave a nervous laugh. 'I wish to. Very much. I am sure I enjoyed the sight of it before and I look forward to seeing it again. But there is no reason to rush.'

'Of course not,' she said, stretching beside him again and pressing a hand to the middle of his chest.

In response, he stroked her hair. 'It is quite embarrassing to admit this, but I do not know if I have the strength to perform. The day has been tiring and I am still weak as a kitten. I am likely to shame myself, should I attempt to be intimate with you.'

When she glanced down, his body said otherwise. She could see the beginnings of arousal growing beneath the bedsheet. 'We will do whatever you wish,' she said, surprised to feel disappointment.

He closed his eyes and sighed, as though it were a relief. Then he said, 'Then we will go where the mood takes us. And I do enjoy your being here, with me. The sound of your voice is soothing. I was told you read to me, while I was unconscious.'

'I did,' she said. 'Only novels. Nothing of substance.' She smiled. 'It seems we share an interest in them.' It had been a chance to indulge a guilty pleasure of her own, while pretending to help him.

'I do not remember the words,' he said. 'But I think I remember the sound of you. You must speak more often for I love to hear it. Your voice is like music.'

'Thank you,' she said.

He closed his eyes, and leaned back into the pillows. 'You have listened to me all night. Now you must speak. Tell me of yourself.'

Her hands froze on his chest and she hoped he did not feel her go rigid with panic. What could she say that might not trigger the very memories she did not want to awaken? 'What do you wish to know?'

'How did you become so clever with your hands? Did your mother teach you?'

She relaxed a little, for that topic was harmless enough. 'It was a skill of hers. But much of the work I taught myself. She was carrying my sister when my father died.' The words almost stuck in her throat and she hurried past them. 'After the birth, she was so very weak.' Memories of her mother were equally painful. 'When Father had been with us, she'd been young and happy. But without him, she'd go days without speaking, staring out of the window of our tiny apartment, her beauty fading a little each year, until the life was gone from her.'

Will must have recognised the fact, for his hand tightened on her shoulder, as if he could lead her away from the past. 'But you still have your sister.'

'Her name is Margot,' she said, relieved. 'She is in school.'

He opened one eye and glanced at her. 'At this time of year?'

'She spends summers and holidays there as well,' Justine said. 'I have no money to help her and must tend to my own work. It is better that she remain there, if there is nowhere for her to stay.'

He had opened both eyes to stare at her now. 'You have somewhere now,' he said, shaking his head in disappointment. 'You are mistress of a house that is more than large enough to hold a young woman, no matter how extravagant her needs might be. Tell me, how old is little Margot?'

'Nearly twenty,' she admitted.

'And still in school?' he said, surprised. 'Is she not out yet?'

'There was no money for a Season.'

'There is now.' He settled back into the pillows again, as though there would be no further discussion. 'She will stay with us until we can arrange for her come out. Let Penny settle everything. She might appear to be a wallflower at times, but she is quite good at organising things. And she is a duchess, after all.'

'Well...' she said, running through the list of reasons that such a trip would be impossible, to search for one that made sense.

Will was staring at her again. 'You want to see her, do you not? There is no estrangement between you?'

'I want to see her more than anything else in the world,' she admitted, feeling the tightness in her heart when she thought of her sister ease a little.

'Then you shall write to her first thing tomorrow and we will have her here, while the weather is still good.'

'Thank you.' She would find a way to change his mind in the morning.

But then it occurred to her that she didn't have to. She could summon Margot and have her in Wales before their guardian knew a thing about it. Once she was part of the duke's family, he could not threaten her or attempt to remove her without admitting who he was. If he attempted it, Justine would threaten to sacrifice herself and reveal what he had done. She did not know much of chess, but she suspected this was what players called a stalemate.

She looked at William Felkirk again, a smile spreading slowly across her face. He had that slightly puzzled expression she associated with men in the jewellery shop who had been surprised when a word or gesture held more significance than the gems they were offering. With one casual suggestion, the man in the bed beside her had the power to reorder her world. 'Thank you.' She said it with more feeling so he might know she was truly grateful. Then, to stop further conversation, she leaned forward and kissed him on the mouth.

She had been kissed often enough. It had been unavoidable. But had *she* ever kissed a man before? Certainly not like this. It was wet and open mouthed, as though her happiness could not be contained behind closed lips. His mouth was surprisingly sweet, as though the ice cream he had rejected was still on his lips. She tasted the flavour. She quite liked it and the feeling of his firm lips against the tip of her tongue.

She could tell her sudden boldness had surprised him. He was still at first. Then his hand settled into the small of her back, drawing her closer to him, pulling her body up on to his chest. Then, everything about him seemed to relax, his mouth falling open against hers, his tongue easing into her mouth to caress hers.

Such kisses had always seemed like an invasion. But this was very different. Will Felkirk's touch was gentle, as though he were learning her from the inside out. She probed gently in response. It was different to respond. She did not feel desire so much as curiosity. What harm would it do to indulge that, as long as it kept him from asking any more questions?

He tasted different. The shape of his mouth was different as well. She could feel the playfulness of his smile, the fullness of his lips and the smoothness of his cheekbone as she stroked it. She moved her hands lower, to his bare chest, which was no longer as sunken and hollow as it had felt while he slept. With a little sunlight and solid food, the health was coming back to him. His heart beat fast and strong under her fingers. She could feel it beating even faster as she touched him. And there, on his arm, was the strange smooth skin of the burn scar.

While she might admit that the duke was the more handsome of the two brothers, he was a trifle too perfect to look at. This man, with the crease in his skull and the scars on his body, was so much more real and she knew him almost too well.

He sighed at her touch and his kisses became a sudden opening and closing of his lips as though he was taking a bite of fruit. Then he sighed again, in satisfaction as if he needed her to feel complete, as one might need air or food.

She stilled for a moment, not sure she liked it. She understood being desired. She understood what it was to be used. She had understood his need when he was too helpless to care for himself. But now the feeling was different. She wanted him to be stronger for her help, not more dependant.

Suppose, when she finally managed to escape from this place, she left him feeling less than whole. She had expected to lose some of herself by this joining. But suppose she grew to depend on him? She could not afford such feelings, if she was ever in her life to be free.

Perhaps it was simply that it had been so long since lying with a man that she had forgotten how to behave. The trick was to disengage one's mind from the activity, so that it might be somewhere else, while the body acted. She tried it now and found it strangely ineffective. The feel of his skin under her hand, was too real to ignore. Instead of hiding from it, she wanted to lose more of herself to him, to be more deeply entwined. In a daring moment, she ran her hand down his chest, following the trail of hair on his belly until it slipped beneath the sheet to grip him.

He inhaled sharply at the touch, taking her tongue more deeply into his mouth.

This was interesting. She had never felt this sense of control before. She took advantage, running a fingertip lightly across the opening at the head of his member.

He pulled away, 'I do not think...' Though his member stirred at her touch, his body moved weakly under hers, a reminder that he was still not fully recovered.

She had but to release him, with an apology for her forwardness. She would be safe from intimacy for another night, or more. Perhaps he would even let her return to her room. Instead, she kissed his lips again and murmured, 'Let me.' Then she moved her hand on him.

As she watched, he settled back into the pillows, but did not relax. His eyes were shut tightly, his mouth shut so tightly that his lips went white. Did her touch hurt him? She thought not, for he made no move to stop her. His nostrils flared as he took a slow steady breath as though struggling to maintain control of his own body and prolong the climax.

Did she really affect him so? The idea that she could award or deny his happiness with a single touch was exhilarating. She gripped him tighter, stroking slowly from root to tip, and felt him growing under her fingers.

He was longer and thicker than she'd expected. Silky skin stretched tight over blood and muscle, growing slippery with the first drops of his seed. She wondered what it would be like when he entered her. Probably not as pleasant as she was imagining. In her experience, real life seldom lived up to imagination.

But the current moment was satisfying enough. As she moved her hand on him, his whole body seemed to tighten, tension building like a coiled spring. His eyes were open again, head had arched back so that he could stare at the ceiling and his lips worked, almost as though praying. In this moment, he was hers in a way that no man had ever been. It made her wish that she could keep him. Or, at least, that she could keep pretending for a lifetime.

She used his vulnerability to kiss his exposed throat, running teeth and tongue along the tendons until she heard the hitch in his breath. Then she released him, just for a second, to raise the hem of her nightdress, brushing him with the picot edging he had found so intriguing.

He shuddered at the contact. She changed her grip, wrapping him in the linen, and tightening her hand to finish him. Beneath her, his whole body jerked and his breath released in a moan. Then, as she had expected, he lost control and sagged helpless back on to the mattress.

She lay still against him, her palm flat against his chest, waiting until he had stopped trembling and his heartbeat began to slow again. Then she rubbed him gently with the linen, rolled away from him and stood to pull the soiled gown over her head and drop it on the floor beside her discarded nightcap.

She glanced at it with a frown. Should she summon a maid, or search in her own bureau for a replacement? She did not normally like sleeping bare. The vulnerability of it was so distressing that she could not rest easy. But tonight felt different. She stretched her arms above her head, noting the pull of muscle and skin, feeling stronger and more confident than before. She smoothed a hand over breast and belly, surprised at how warm they felt. Then she turned towards the connecting door between the rooms.

'Stay.'

She looked back at Will, surprised. How could she have forgotten that he was there, just behind her, watching this shameless display of her body?

But she had nothing to fear. There was no avarice

in his gaze. His look held more wonder than lust. He reached out a hand to her, as though to stop her departure. 'Come back to bed. We need do nothing more. But sleep here tonight, at my side.'

'Very well,' she said. She came back to the bed and climbed beneath the covers, letting him gather her close. In less than a sigh, he was asleep.

She lay awake beside him, surprised at how relaxing it was to share a bed with William Felkirk. She dreaded those nights that Montague expected it of her, for it invariably meant that she would be wakened at some point and required to service him.

But judging by the slight snore that escaped his parted lips, the man at her side now was not likely to wake. His arm wrapped loosely around her, his thigh brushing her leg. But the limbs were as relaxed and heavy as they had been as he'd lain in a coma.

This feeling of skin against skin was a new thing as well. She ought to be frightened, lying hip to hip with a stranger. But this was more decadent than disturbing. She yawned. Perhaps this was what it was like to be a courtesan, taking and discarding lovers without a second thought.

Or perhaps it was how she'd have felt, had she been a wife.

The thought was gone as quickly as it had come, for she was slipping away, into a dark and peaceful sleep.

Chapter Ten

When Will awoke the next morning, she was gone from his bed. Perhaps last night's release was what he had needed. It was the first real rest he'd had since waking from the coma. He'd slept so soundly that he had no idea whether she'd stayed as he asked.

He rather hoped she had. His dreams had been deliciously lurid, opium-drenched fantasies of some Turkish paradise where he reclined on a pillow while a nubile woman ministered to his every need.

He grinned. What he had thought of as a dream was very close to what had actually happened. She had seemed so prim when she came to him in her plain gown and cap. Then she had kissed him soundly and taken him to heaven with a single hand. After, she'd stripped naked at his bedside and stretched like a satisfied cat.

Was it any wonder that he had dreamed of paradise? When he closed his eyes he could still see her high, full breasts bobbing above a narrow waist and hips that made a man long to hold on to them. What had he been thinking, to invite her to bed so that they might simply talk? She had pleasured him to the point where it had not mattered in the slightest who she was or where she'd come from. His only concern had been that she continue until she had finished.

When he came down to breakfast, she was already there. He should not have been surprised. He thought himself an early riser, but she seemed to pride herself on being ahead of him. The post had come and she had kept a single letter for herself and arranged the rest at his place. Then she made sure that his plate and cup were prepared just as he would like it.

Today, instead of greeting her with a curt nod, he went to her side and kissed her lightly on the cheek. He glanced down at the paper in front of her.

He frowned. Despite what had happened between them, she still seemed to stiffen at the touch of his lips and shift nervously away as though fearing a blow. Her movement obscured the note, which had all but disappeared beneath her plate. Then she relaxed into the passive doll he had come to expect. 'Good morning, William,' she said dutifully.

'And good morning to you, my dear.' *And where have you gone?* It was not as if he expected her to arrive at the table like a slave in a harem, attired in nothing but scarves. But when he looked at her, he'd expected to find some sign of the change between them.

She glanced down at the paper peeping out from beneath her breakfast plate. 'If you are wondering about the letter, it is a note from a friend of my parents, congratulating me upon our marriage. I will answer it after breakfast.'

'Of course,' he said. It was not so unusual that she had friends, nor that they would correspond with her. But since she had not mentioned them before, he had flattered himself that he was her entire world. It did him no credit that he felt jealous of the person who wrote to her and the time she would spend on them. 'And you will write to your sister as we discussed?'

Her expression, which had been pensive, changed to a brief, radiant smile. Then it faded to the more sedate half-smile she usually wore. 'If you still wish me to, I would like that.'

It was as if the sun had come out from behind a cloud only to disappear again. He grinned at her, hoping to remind her of the previous night. 'Of course I still wish it. And if there is anything else that will make you smile as you have just done, you must ask immediately. On such a fine morning as this, I could deny you nothing.'

She glanced at the window, as though expecting to see a change in the weather. 'I thought it rather chill, when I was walking.' She looked back at him, giving no indication that she understood the reason for his happiness could be traced back to last night. She held out his cup, 'Coffee?'

He took his usual seat and accepted the cup.

'Thank you.' Perhaps it was an ordinary thing for her, or had been so before the accident. If that was true, then damn him for forgetting so much. He leaned closer to her, catching her eye and smiling. 'And thank you for last night as well.'

The delightful pink of her cheeks clashed with the reds in her hair. 'You are welcome.' She glanced down at the table. Toast?' She pushed the toast rack closer to his plate, as though appeasing one appetite would make him forget the other.

He ignored her offer of bread and continued on his original topic. 'I enjoyed what you did for me, very much,' he said, thinking the words oddly polite. But they seemed a match for her reserved response.

'I am glad,' she said, sending the marmalade pot after the toast with a nudge of her finger.

He ignored that as well. 'Did you enjoy it as well?'

To this, she gave him an odd look, as though it had not occurred to her to have an opinion about it. 'It makes me happy when you are happy.' Then the placid smile returned.

'That is not what I asked,' he said. 'I want to know if you enjoyed touching me.'

She glanced around her, as if to remind him that they were in the breakfast room, not the bedroom. She looked down at her plate as though trying to decide if it might be possible to pretend she had not heard. She took up her knife and fork and began slicing the sausage on it into ever smaller bites. Then, as if she'd noticed what she had done to the rather significantly shaped meat, she set down her utensils with a clatter and said, in a rush of words, 'Enjoyed it? Of course. Why should I not? You are my husband, after all, and it is my goal...'

'To make me happy,' he finished. 'That brings us back to where we began.' He pushed the toast rack out of the way and reached for one of her hands, holding it gently in his and noticing how cold the fingers were. 'It is not that I object to being happy. But I assume, when I married you, that I wanted you to be happy as well. Surely I said something of the kind.' He hoped that it was true. This morning, she was acting almost as if she was afraid of him.

She blinked at him, as though the details of their past were as murky to her as they were to him. Then she glanced down at their joined hands with an expression of such modesty and beauty that he wanted to capture it in oils. 'Of course, my love. It is just that I do not want to seem less than grateful for all you and your family have done for me. Your offer last night, to allow me to send for Margot...' She looked up hopefully, as though fearing he meant to retract it in the cold light of day.

'Grateful?' Was that why she had been so affectionate? It was oddly annoying to think that her treatment of him had been some sort of a reward for a perfectly normal offer of hospitality. 'You needn't be, over such a small thing. Where else would you sister stay, if not with us? If you pine for her company, then you shall have it.'

'I do. Very much so.' Her smile returned, and for a moment he was afraid that she might cry. Or stranger still, that she might repeat her behaviour of the previous evening and sink to her knees before him during breakfast. Exciting though the idea was, it was rather alarming to think of her putting a hand in his breeches each time she wanted a favour.

'Then it is what I wish as well,' he said carefully. 'For I want to see you happy, just as you wish to see me happy.'

She nodded, as though all was settled.

'But I wish that your happiness, last night and in nights to come, can be separate from the thought of your sister's visit. It is quite a different thing, you see.'

'Of course it is,' she said, nodding. But there was something in her tone that announced she had no idea what he was talking about. What kind of a selfish beast had he been, if he had not taught her that the bedroom was a place to seek mutual pleasure? This obtuse behaviour on her part was almost enough to set his mind to doubting again. It did not sound like him, at all.

At least, it did not sound like the sort of husband and lover he had wished to be. But how was he to know, really? His experience thus far had been limited to the sort of women who knew what they wanted in bed, even if it was only to pretend satisfaction in exchange for jewellery and rent.

Did gently bred virgins behave in the same way?

Were they taught to submit to their husbands and trade favour for favour like courtesans? Did no one speak to them of the pleasure of the act? Perhaps it was his job to teach that particular lesson. The prospect of that made him want to grin like an idiot. Instead, he smiled at her with as much kindness and gentleness as he could muster, then leaned forward to kiss her on the cheek again. 'Tonight, I shall demonstrate what I mean.'

'Oh.' It was but one word. But she said it in a tone that said, *oh, dear.* Or, worse yet, *oh dear, you needn't bother.* If he had not seen her on the previous evening, totally in control of both his body and her own nerves, he'd have thought she was frightened.

'For now, let us finish our breakfast,' he said, dismissing the subject until later. 'I will leave you alone so you might go to the morning room and write letters to your friend and to your sister.'

With that, the relieved smile returned to her face as though it had never left.

He expected something of her.

Justine was not sure what it was that he had wanted, but it seemed some display of happiness was in order. Clearly, he did not understand how difficult it was to appear pleasant and at ease when one was already holding a paper full of admonishments on how she must behave if she was to ferret out the Felkirk family secrets. In his note, Montague had approved of the move to this house, since it was most likely to hold what they were looking for.

But he had also hinted that he would expect a detailed accounting of her activities when next they met in the woods. She rather feared that was more than just a description of the rooms she had searched and what she might have uncovered in them. He would want to know exactly what had transpired in the bedroom with Will.

Of course, Will seemed to want to talk of that as well. What was wrong with men, that they could not put what happened in the bedroom firmly in the past, as she meant to do? His kisses were nice, of course. She especially liked the little ones he had given her in the breakfast room, as though it were a matter of course to remind her of his feelings throughout the day.

But she wished he would stop. Small kisses only made her think of other, more intimate ones and the feel of his skin under her hand. It felt nice, just as the kisses did. But it would all lead to the same place in the end, where he had all the control and she had none. Badgering her about her own happiness was unnecessary. Life was what it was. Even the difficult bits went more smoothly if one did not brood on one's feelings from moment to moment.

This morning, he meant to leave her alone, just as promised, to write her letters. Once the door was closed, she began with a thorough examination of the room. As she'd expected, she did not find a desk drawer full of loose stones, or a treasure map rolled up in a pigeon hole. Yesterday's tour of the house had convinced her that the library was the only room worth searching. It held the books and papers left behind when the previous duke had moved to the new house.

If there was nothing to be found, so be it. She assured Montague in the note she wrote him that she would follow his orders to the letter, but she had no real intention of rooting through Will Felkirk's mind for the truth. Why risk disturbing the conveniently forgotten past, on the slim hope of gain?

It was far better, in her opinion, to ensure Margot's safety through the rather ordinary method Will had suggested. If money was needed to make her situation permanent, she did not need stolen diamonds. Her husband was a most agreeable man. If he meant what he'd said at breakfast, she had but to smile and ask for it, and he would open his purse and give her whatever she needed. It would work for a time, at least. Justine would face the consequences if and when he remembered what had happened in Bath. With luck, Margot might be safely married before the truth came out.

But the first step towards that happy state was to invite her sister for a visit. Justine chewed on her pen, unsure of what to say. There was so much that had happened and so little that could be explained. Suppose someone at the school saw the letter, or enquired as to the reasons for Margot's sudden departure. Suppose Montague had spies to prevent Margot's escape from his power. She must not think of that. There was little she could do, other than to hope that Montague heard nothing until Margot was well under way.

In the end, she settled on a brief note, explaining that she had married and was eager for her sister's company. Margot was cautioned to tell no one of the wedding, as it had not been announced to the whole of William's family. Under no circumstances was she to communicate with Mr Montague, as it was a sudden elopement and Justine had yet to tell him of it. If anyone asked, she must simply say that she had been called home for a visit. Then she was to take the next carriage north. Once she was here, all would be explained.

She folded sufficient bank notes in the letter to allow for comfortable travel, sealed it up and summoned a footman to place it and the note to Montague in the outgoing post. Now she had but to hope that Margot appeared before her next visit with her guardian.

Will was secretly relieved that Justine had plans to occupy herself for the morning. If she had taken such care in nursing him to health, he doubted that she would approve of what he had planned for his day. If one wished to regain one's life, some risk must be taken. He had no plans to remain swaddled in cotton wool, simply to please his lady.

His lady. The idea was more appealing than it had

been, just a day ago. There were still problems, of course. But many of them involved coaxing his wife out of the shell she had built around herself.

His own problems would be dealt with as they arose. He meant to conquer the first one today. He walked out from the house, choosing a stouter walking stick than usual, in case he became unsteady. Though he tired easily, and had to rest once on his way, there were no instances of imbalance. While he did not feel as strong as a bull, he could almost forget that he had recently been an invalid.

His nose pricked at the scent of hay and horse, growing stronger with each step. Justine would laugh at him, should he tell her that the smell of manure was its own sort of cure. But it reminded him of how he felt in the saddle, riding a beast that was the epitome of strength and freedom. He paused at the doorway, offering a brief prayer, should anything remain of the spirit of his faithful Jupiter. If there was a heaven, Will's place there must have a stall for Jupe.

He paused again, staring into the barn and allowing his eyes to adjust to the dim light within. Then he ignored the sadness and carefully searched his heart for any signs of fear. He had been telling himself it was his own foolhardiness that had nearly killed him. A weaker man might have blamed the horse that failed him. Of course, a stronger man would have had the sense not to take a jump. Could he really trust his own mind at all?

'Hello, my lord,' the stable master said.

'Hello, Jenks.' Jenks was technically a servant of the duke's, but he had been with the family since Will and Adam were boys. The man had taught him to ride. Who better to understand the problems that might occur today? 'I suppose you heard of my accident?'

'Yes, my lord. We were all most concerned for you.'

'I cannot remember much of what happened.' It was a lie. But it was too painful to own the total blank of the incident. 'It seems I lost my mount as well.'

'A shame, my lord.' There was no censure in the voice, even though he deserved it. 'Are you planning a trip to Tattersall's?'

Will sighed. 'I do not know if I am ready to purchase another. But I must get a horse under me, sooner rather than later. If there is a problem with my judgement...' For instance, if he collapsed in terror before taking the saddle. He had known of a man so shaken after a little tumble that he had sold his hunter and now travelled in nothing more exciting than a barouche with full livery.

Jenks nodded again. 'It is widely said, sir, that when one falls, one must get right back on.'

'It is almost a cliché,' Will agreed, 'but very true. What do you have ready in the stalls for me? I fancy a gentle ride about the property.' He had emphasised the word gentle, but just the sound of it depressed him.

'If you wish a gentle ride, I have a mare right

here, ready to saddle.' Jenks patted the neck of a nearby grey and her head swung round slowly to look at them.

Will had expected fixed feelings, when the moment came to ride again. Perhaps he would not experience outright terror. At least there would be some trepidation at mounting. However, at the sight of the horse Jenks suggested, he felt nothing but scorn. 'You might as well put a saddle on Penny's pet terrier. It would have more spirit than this beast.'

There was a sparkle in Jenks's eye, as though he had meant the first choice as nothing more than a joke. He walked down the row of stalls, and stopped before a chestnut gelding. 'Perhaps Aries will suit you better. Sound legs. A good chest. Not prone to starts or skittishness. He is a fine horse, my lord.'

'True.' He could handle the beast easily. But somehow, the thought of riding did not excite him as it once did. He glanced down the row at the largest stall, a place of honour in the centre of the stable. 'Do you think my brother would mind if I borrowed Zeus?'

Jenks started in surprise. 'He would not mind, for the beast needs exercise. But do you think it wise?' Zeus was black as Satan and notoriously bad tempered. But he shared a sire with Jupiter and was as close as Will was likely to get to his old friend.

'It is probably not the best decision,' Will admitted. 'But I would like to try. Keeping control of him will teach me to be alert, when in the saddle.'

'Of course, my lord.' Jenks gave him a doubtful look, but set about saddling the horse. And, as Zeus was wont to do, he spat out the bit, blew out his stomach to fight the saddling and danced in the stall, making it as hard as possible to accomplish the task.

The sight should have worried him. If he had nearly split his head after a ride, shouldn't such a spirited animal worry him? Instead, when he looked at Zeus, he felt excited and eager to ride. It had been too long since he had felt a horse under him. When Jenks finally got control of the stallion and led him out of the stable, Will practically itched with the desire to mount.

It was not as easy as he'd hoped. His legs were still weak and he had to resort to a mounting block to get a foot into the stirrup. But once he was astride, the problems were minimal and he set out from the stable at a walk.

It was good to feel the wind in his face again and good to see the family lands from the accustomed combined height of man and animal. He glanced back at his house, hoping that Justine was not too near any of the windows, as he did not want to frighten her, then nudged the horse to a trot. There was still no sign of the fear he had expected to find in himself. Other than the strangeness of a new mount, there was nothing exceptionable about the ride.

He experimented with cantering, and even galloped for a short stretch with similar results. Zeus seemed more bothered by the outing than he, he recognised that the commands he was given were not from his true master and was still trying to decide whether he needed to obey them. But Will kept a firm hand on the reigns and tightened the grip of his thighs which, if truth be told, were still not strong enough to take too much more of this.

One last test and he would go back to the stables. He turned the horse towards a low fence at the bottom of the pasture. There was no risk in it. He had been jumping that particular obstacle since he was a boy and the horse was familiar with it as well. As they approached, he felt nothing but pleasant anticipation of both man and beast, for the moment of weightless flight as they passed over it. And they did, with ease.

It was then that Zeus chose his moment for rebellion, landing hard, dipping his head and digging in his feet to send Will over his neck and to the ground with a thump. His moment of triumph was immediately followed by the air being jarred out of his lungs and the warning snap of large sharp teeth beside his ear.

'You dirty bastard,' he wheezed, rolling out of the way.

'My lord!' Jenks was rushing to his side to take the reins and help him to his feet.

Will held up a hand to signify that all was well and managed a weak laugh. 'Nothing to worry about, Jenks. I have not cracked my pate, or damaged anything but my dignity.' Hardly even that. The fall had been tonic, just as the ride had been. He had not feared the jump or the fall. His riding clothes were stained with mud and he smelled of grass and dried leaves. But he had not shattered as he'd feared he might. His mistake had been in taking his brother's miserable horse out in the first place. But there was nothing particularly fragile about him that might prevent such rides in the future.

He thanked Jenks for his help and promised to visit again soon and choose a more manageable horse. Other than that, the day had been a success. Yet it did not fully content him. Would he never regain anything from the time before the accident?

It was sad that he could not remember his wife. But how near to death did one need to go to erase even the fear of falling from one's mind? He had been half-expecting that an innocent tumble would knock the memory back into him. He would see a flash of that time, on a different horse. Perhaps Jupe had startled at the sight of a rabbit, or stumbled on a hole. He had sent Will sailing through the air with the knowledge that the landing was likely to be a bad one, ending in pain and darkness.

Still, there was nothing. His mind was as smooth and as blank as a block of ice, with the things he wanted frozen for ever inside. He would find Justine and beg her for more information on the day of his accident. Perhaps she had seen something that might have indicated the reason for it, other than carelessness on his part. Had he been drunk, or in some other way completely unaware of what was about to happen to him?

When he returned to the house, she was nowhere to be found. The morning room was as tidy as if she had never occupied it at all. Her bedroom was equally empty, as was his. Only in the library did he see evidence of her presence. In the darkest corner of the room, a table was stacked with leather-bound journals his mother had kept while she still lived in the house. What she sought there, he was not sure, for his mother had been an indifferent correspondent at best.

Beside them, the family Bible was open to the page where his birth had been recorded, along with the significant events of his childhood. Was she really so eager to please him that she chose to research his past? What else could she be looking for but his mother's anecdotal record of his life and perhaps a few favourite recipes and menus?

He smiled. He'd have found the behaviour strange, had it been described to him. But there was so much about his new wife that was odd, it hardly surprised him. If she had a fault, it was her almost obsessive desire to make him happy. Tonight, she would be surprised to learn that to accomplish her goal she must take as much pleasure as she gave.

Chapter Eleven

Justine pulled a row of pins and undid the last few knots of the lace on her pillow, so that she might fix the mistakes she'd made when she'd lost concentration. Perhaps she should ask Will to read Walter Scott tonight, especially the bit about tangled webs and deception. Of course, a dishonest woman in that story had ended up walled alive in an abbey. In her current frame of mind, that story would not be light entertainment.

'You are sure there is nothing you can recall about the accident that might make things clearer.'

Since she was making the story up as she went, she doubted that she had the detail he was hoping for. 'I was not close enough to see. And it all happened too fast.' He had been questioning her all through dinner about the past. After nearly two hours, he was no closer to what he expected to hear, but she balanced on the edge of a knife.

He was silent for a moment and she took the opportunity to turn the tables on him. 'In my opinion, it is fortunate that you do not remember. Suppose it had come upon you suddenly and given you a turn. It was very dangerous to ride at all. What if something had happened and you had fallen again?'

Now he was the one who was uncomfortable, squirming in his seat like a guilty little boy.

She looked up from her work, too surprised to remember the role she was playing. 'You fell again, didn't you?'

'It was nothing,' he replied hurriedly. 'I was back on my feet as soon as I regained my wind. But it makes me all the more confused at what caused the earlier accident.'

'I do not know why I bothered to nurse you, if you use your recovery foolishly.' Was this real alarm she was feeling at the thought of him lying hurt again? It was always sad when a man so young and alive met with a tragic accident. But when had it begun to matter to her?

He was at her side now, full of apology. 'If it bothers you, I will take no more chances. Adam's horse is a brute. I will not take him out again.' He knelt in front of her now, until he was sure that he had caught her eye. 'Am I forgiven?'

'Of course,' she said, trying and failing for her usual calm smile.

'Very good,' he said, then stared down at the work in her lap. She resumed her knotting, and he watched, fascinated by the rhythmic click and switch of the bone bobbins, the exactitude of pins and the slow but steady increase in finished work. 'What are you making?' he asked at last, unable to contain his curiosity.

'I do not know, as of yet,' she said. 'A bit of trim for something. It is an old pattern and I do not have to think to work it. But it makes up very pretty.'

'If you do not know what it is for, then why are you doing it?'

'To keep my hands busy,' she said. 'Idle hands are the devil's playthings, after all.'

'Have you given thought to my suggestion of last night?'

She frowned, trying to remember what it was that he had said.

'When I told you to make something for yourself,' he said. 'A tucker for that bodice, perhaps.' He was staring at her breasts.

She placed a hand on her chest to hide them. 'I am sorry if the gown is too low. I will change, if you wish.'

He pulled her hand away, wrapping the fingers with his. 'There is nothing wrong with the dress, other than that it is rather plain. Not that you need to adorn yourself, to be more beautiful,' he added hurriedly. 'It simply surprises me that you do not treat yourself as you do others.'

She nodded, relieved that she had done nothing to offend. 'It is such a large amount of work, if it is only to go for me.'

He thought for a moment. 'Then you must make something for me,' he said.

At this, she let out one small laugh, before stifling the emotion so as not to seem disagreeable. 'Now you are being silly. Men do not wear lace such as this.'

He walked to her side and reached into her work basket, removing a particularly feminine scrap and draping it over his wrist. 'Perhaps I shall create a fashion for it. Can you not see me in a neckcloth trimmed in birds and butterflies?'

'I cannot,' she said, without looking up.

'Then you must make something for yourself, as a gift for me. I wish to see you adorned in lace, as I said last night.' Then he draped it over the bare skin of her shoulder, admiring the flesh through the holes in the cloth.

The gentle brush on her shoulder seemed to strike at the very heart of her. Her breath caught in her throat and the room seemed strangely warm. She shrugged to get free of it. 'I do not think it would suit me.'

'It is not as beautiful as you are,' he admitted. 'But it is lovely all the same.'

This time, it was his words that stopped her breath. He had complimented her before. Why did it matter now?

He trailed the lace up the length of her arm. 'When we married, did you not promise to obey?'

'Yes.' She almost whispered the word. Even for this man, would she ever have the courage to make such a promise, knowing what it might entail?

He smiled, triumphant. 'Then I should like to see you wear lace. Not all the time. But often enough to prove you understand your own worth. If you will not make it for yourself, I shall buy it for you. Yards and yards of it.'

'Now, that is certainly a waste,' she said, imagining what such foolishness was likely to cost, compared with the work she might do for the cost of thread, was she willing to take the time.

'It would be worth it to me,' he said, 'if it meant that I might see you dressed head to toe in nothing but that.'

If the idea had ever occurred to her before, she had set it aside as the kind of sinfully decadent thing a kept woman might do. That was reason enough to avoid it. It was less pleasant than one might expect to spend days parading about the shop in jewels like a mannequin brought to life. It was even worse to spend her evenings dressed as an object of desire.

But that had been when she was with Montague. Why was it strangely appealing when the man making the request was Will Felkirk? 'It would not be very practical,' she said at last. 'Too likely to tear.'

'I would remove it carefully,' he assured her.

Her heart was beating fast now and she could feel her skin flushing, as though she was already displayed before him in a transparent gown. 'It would take months to make a whole chemise,' she said, hoping that might settle the matter.

He pretended to frown at this. But she could see

the smile playing at the corner of his lips, as though her perfectly sensible response had amused him. Then he trailed the lace lightly across the back of her hand, up her arm and away, to hold it in front of her face. 'Perhaps you could make a veil.' He peered through it at her. 'Did you wear one at our wedding?'

'No,' she whispered.

He nodded, 'Because you had nothing to hide. But I can imagine it, all the same.' He dragged the lace across her face, covering her eyes like a mask. Then he lowered it to cover her mouth. 'Do you know there are cultures in the East where women hide their faces beneath veils from all but their husbands?' He raised his eyes above the edge and gave her an arch look.

'You would not expect that of me,' she said, surprised.

'It would be selfish of me to obscure such a face,' he said. 'Besides, you are almost too modest already, without my encouraging. You have no idea how arousing it is to see you so prim and proper, knowing what you keep concealed beneath your gown.' He sighed then and kissed her through the lace. It was worthy of the innocence of the decoration, a simple touch of lip to lip through the barrier that separated them. There was nothing dangerous or demanding about it.

But her reaction to it was a surprise. She pressed her mouth into the fabric in eager response, her tongue licking at it as though she expected it to dissolve like spun sugar. That was what she wanted.

A hint of sweetness, then a long, hot, meeting of mouths and tongues.

Did he share her feelings? Perhaps not. He lingered there, for a moment, then pressed a closed-mouthed kiss on to each of her closed eyes before dropping the lace back into the basket.

He smiled, as if he had discovered a secret. 'It is just as I thought. Your beauty does not need gilding, but a touch of your own handiwork makes you all the more alluring. Now promise me that the next thing you make will be a gift for yourself.'

'Yes,' she whispered. It was an answer to a question he had not asked.

'Very good,' he said and stood up again. Then he yawned as he had the previous evening. 'And now, if you don't mind, this conversation has put me in a mood to retire early.' Perhaps he had understood, for the smile he gave her was warm and so full of confidence that it made her blush. 'You may join me at your leisure.' When he turned to leave, he barely needed the support of his cane.

She waited until she was sure he had gained the stairs before beginning to pack up her work for the night. She would lie with him tonight, if he wished it. She could not play the role of wife to him without submitting to his desires. It was what he expected. Montague expected it as well. But what had she wanted, when she had first come here?

Nothing more than to be left alone. She wanted to be able to decide for herself what her future held. Instead, she had become an obedient servant to another man. He was kinder than the first. More handsome as well. They shared interests. And they understood each other, or would, if she allowed him to know more of her.

But if she allowed him to know all? Then whatever they shared would be over, as quickly as it had begun. His gentle seduction and caring ways would disappear once he realised that she was another man's cast off. Worse yet, that she was still that man's property, set in Will's house as a spy.

She set the needlework basket beneath her chair, where it would be ready for the next night. She took one last glance at the bit of lace that Will had held, before closing the top of the basket to hide it. It would be wise to shut her dreams away as well, for they would only lead to heartbreak in the end. She would lie with him tonight, as he expected. He deserved her obedience for what he was doing to help Margot, even if he did not understand the urgency of it. But there was no point in investing the act with hopes and plans that would all come to nothing.

Chapter Twelve

She went to her room and summoned the maid to prepare her for bed. She looked at the simple gown laid out for her and thought with distaste of the more daring garments she had left behind in Bath. It was something of that sort that Will expected to see. If this charade continued, she would purchase new ones that were free of memories of her old life.

She donned the gown and refused the nightcap, since he had expressed his dislike of it the previous evening, and requested only a loose braid in her hair. All things would be as he wished. Then she dismissed her maid and went through the door connecting their rooms, shutting it softly behind her.

Tonight, he was just as he had been the night before, leaning against the headboard and waiting for her. He smiled as she entered the room, and moved on the mattress to give her space. As she approached, he gave a single disappointed glance at the gown she was wearing.

Without a second thought, she removed it, draped it over the foot of the bed and climbed naked into the bed beside him. Then she very deliberately rubbed her bare leg against his in a way guaranteed to arouse him.

She felt him start and pull away. For a moment, it almost seemed that he would climb from the opposite side of the bed to get away from her.

She made to withdraw. 'If you do not want…'

'No,' he said. 'I mean, yes. Stay. Just like this.' He had relaxed again, drawing her closer, wrapping his arms about her so her breasts pressed into his side. 'It is just that, as I have told you before, there is no need to rush.'

'Oh,' she said, trying not to sound vexed. In her opinion, just the opposite was true. The sooner they were done, the sooner she could put aside the disquieting feelings he raised in her, and restore peace to her mind.

He took a breath. 'And I must be truthful. After last night, I am somewhat concerned about the way things might proceed this evening.'

'Did I do something to displease you?' she said, searching her brain for an answer.

'No,' he said hurriedly and touched her chin with a fingertip, tipping her head up to offer a long, slow kiss. When they parted, he spoke again. 'Perhaps I did not make myself clear this morning. Last night, you were all I could have hoped for. It is obvious that you know how to pleasure me.'

She nodded in agreement. She had taken a portion of the day to search his rooms for some clue to the diamonds. She had found nothing exceptional, other than a collection of rather risqué etchings in the table by the bedside, that might serve as instruction should she need to maintain his interest in her.

'I am ashamed for ever doubting you,' he said. 'Your beauty is unparallelled. Your devotion to me unwavering. And last night? Your touch was heaven. Though I cannot remember what was in our past, I have no trouble imagining our future together.'

'Then you have no reason for concern,' she said, trying to empty her mind of anything but the moment. Tempting as it was, she dare not think such things herself. If she stayed, disaster was almost inevitable. But there was something very unnerving about the way he reached to the core of her heart when he spoke.

'I do,' he insisted. 'While you know just what it is that I enjoy, I still cannot remember the details of our life together.'

'What do you wish to know?'

'For example, I do not know if you prefer the left side of the bed, or the right.'

'The left,' she said automatically. Then she remembered that it would have been better to allow him to choose.

'Which is where you are now,' he said, satisfied. 'Perhaps I do remember, for it feels very natural to have you here.'

He was probably confusing her with someone else who had shared his bed. The thought was strangely annoying. But if he was happy, then what did it matter?

'And last night,' he said cautiously. 'We have done that before, I assume.'

'Something similar,' she admitted, not wanting to think how she had gained her knowledge of the male anatomy.

'It has been some time since I have truly felt myself. You must forgive me if, for any reason, I am not the man I was.'

'It will not matter,' she said and then lied through her teeth. 'You are still my husband.'

'As your husband, I owe you what you have given to me,' he said firmly. 'I am sorry,' he said with a sad smile, 'that I cannot remember the details of it.'

The conversation was beginning to worry her. If their bed became a place for talk, and the sharing of secrets, she would soon make a slip that could not be explained away. Better to distract him with her body, as she had last night, and save conversation for breakfast, when she had her wits about her. 'The past does not matter,' she said. 'Only the present. And your happiness.' She gave him what she hoped was an encouraging kiss and ran a hand down his body to be sure he was ready. Then, she stretched out on her back, legs sprawled, waiting.

He remained, propped on his elbow, watching her. Then he cleared his throat. 'This is embarrassing to admit. But you will know soon enough, so I had best simply put it out there. I do not remember how to love you.' He had paused before he said it, sounding almost sincere in his apprehension.

She rolled on to her elbow to stare back at him.

'You have forgotten how to…' Was that even a thing that could be forgotten? How was she to describe it to him without resulting to crass gestures and words that no lady should know?

He laughed, relaxed on to the mattress and reached for her, rolling her so that her body was on top of his. The suddenness of it left her breathless. 'Clearly, I married you not for your extreme beauty, but for your sense of humour. I am not so damaged that I could forget that, Justine. And you should know by now that some parts of the act are autonomic.'

He meant the erection pressing into her belly as she moved on top of him. As she slid her bare leg against his it grew even harder. She felt a sudden, nervous swooping in the pit of her stomach, at the thought of it, sliding into her body. She wet her lips. 'I am aware of that.'

'My response to you is not at issue. You are a beautiful woman. If there is strength in my body to act at all, I will know how to take pleasure in you.'

She nodded. What man did not know how to take from a woman, without thinking?

He smiled and kissed her again, short and quick. 'What I do not remember is how to make love to you. As opposed to some other woman, I mean. I do not remember the things that are most important, the things that make you different from all others. I have forgotten how to give you pleasure.'

Help my sister. Give me the diamonds. Let me leave. Those things above all others would be the best way to make her happy. But that was not what he was wondering about. 'If you are pleased, then I shall be as well,' she said, straddling him and hoping that this would be enough to end the talking so that they might commence and be done with it, before she lost her nerve. She gave a nudge with her hips, then she set about clearing her mind, forcing herself to relax so that he might enter her easily. Better to think of nothing at all, during the act, than the disquieting thoughts he insisted on raising in her. She wanted to be in another world entirely: a garden, the sea. Anywhere but in a bed feeling lips and skin, and the loss of her own will.

Still, he did not move, other than to shift the thing growing between them to a more comfortable position. 'Anything I like?' he repeated, with a sigh. 'So you said, last night. And this morning as well. While what happened last night was very nice—'

She frowned. It had been better than nice. She had been sure of it.

'—tonight, I am seeking mutual pleasure.' He gave her a wicked grin. 'Ladies first, as they say. Now, where would you like me to start?'

She closed her eyes tight, not wanting to see his expectant look. He could not possibly understand what he was asking of her. It was taking all her skill to remain calm and not succumb to the things he wished from her. Did she truly have to explain to him that kisses and petting were unnecessary, once they had got to this stage? Did he mean to paw at her breasts, trying to arouse her before pushing himself into her and having his way? To feel pleasure from such a thing, when one had no choice in partners, was the definition of defeat.

'My elbow,' she said, hoping that the sarcasm would put a stop to the questions.

'Your elbow.' Without hesitation, he reached for her arm.

She pulled it away. 'The left one. Not the right.'

He laughed. 'I do not know how I could have forgotten.' He cupped it in his palm and yanked her forward, so she was stretched the length of his body. Then he pulled her bent arm to his lips.

'What are you doing?' she said, unsure whether to laugh or scream. But it was obvious what he was doing. His tongue was circling the little round knob of bone now, as his whole mouth closed over it, sucking and laving as though it were her nipple.

'Exactly what you asked,' he said, blowing on the skin. 'Although it hardly seems fair to ignore your other arm.' His fingers were toying with that, giving a sharp pinch before running the nail lightly back and forth along the skin.

It was too ridiculous to be angry with him. And to her surprise, it was rather pleasant. When he pressed in a certain way, there was an occasional tingle of the nerves beneath that made her breasts tighten as they rubbed against the hair on his chest.

He paused. 'Was that what you meant? Or perhaps you meant the inside of your arm,' He turned his head and buried it in the crook of her arm.

Now this was something quite different. The deep, open-mouthed contact reminded her of something. One of the pictures in the etching book had held her attention for some time. A man's head rested between a woman's legs. He could not be emulating that, could he?

But he was the one who had the book. And he was nipping at the skin of her arm as though trying to take a pinch of it between his teeth. Now his tongue was working, probing, hard against soft, as though he meant to lose himself in her flesh...

'Oh, God.' Had she actually said that and in such a gasping, desperate voice? Because at the thought of his tongue, and what it could do, she was as wet between her legs as if he had licked her. His member rested between her thighs and she squirmed against it, not sure if she was trying to resist or encourage. 'I was not serious,' she whispered, wishing he would stop, but fearing it as well.

He paused for a moment, looking up at her with a smile. 'I know. But a woman who teases will be teased in return. It is fair, is it not?' He rested a thumb where his mouth had been and turned to her right arm.

She moaned in response and circled her hips, rubbing against him to spread the moisture and the sensations that came with it. It was not supposed to be like this. She was sure of it. The detachment she needed to maintain her sanity was melting like spring snow.

She was losing her mind over nothing at all. The only contact between the most intimate parts of their bodies was the result of her urging. And urge she did, wanting desperately to break his resolve as she had last night.

He paused again, dropping a brief kiss on to the skin of her forearm. 'My memory returns, I think. You like this as well, do you not?' Suddenly, he dropped his hands to her legs and pulled them up, until her body spread over his. Then he ran his fingers slowly over the skin at the back of her bent knees.

She gripped the pillow on either side of his head with clenched fists. Of their own volition, her hips bucked against his. His touch should be harmless, but her body was on fire, burning up with the need to be filled. And still he did not advance.

She forgot her need to be passive, the importance of compliance and the need to keep herself apart and safe. She released the pillow and tangled her fingers in his hair, pulling his mouth to hers. But he continued to tease her, running the tip of his tongue along the edge of her teeth and going no further. His fingers played at the back of her legs, stroking at the crease in the skin until all she could think of was his hand between her legs.

She rubbed her body against his, needing the contact, the touch of his tip against the nub of pleasure hidden in the folds of her body. And suddenly she was as far away from her fears as she had ever longed to be. There was no peace here, no separation from the needs of her body. There was only the wildest kind of pleasure, pounding blood, beating heart and the trembling of each ecstatic muscle. Somewhere, in a very distant place, she was begging for more, calling him her beloved, Will, William, Will.

When he was slow to respond, she pushed away from him, reached down, gripped his manhood and impaled herself on it, soaring even higher as he thrust within her. She held him close with arms and legs and the very centre of her being.

When had she ever felt like this before? It was if her body was one with his, feeling that rush of release that men seemed to crave above all things. He was already spent when she came back to earth again, sinking slowly down the length with a sigh, too weak to move.

He took the opportunity to roll her to the left side of the bed again, the one she preferred. Then he followed her, burying his face against her breasts and taking the nipples into his mouth, licking and sucking. His fingertips played over her body with featherlight touches, stroking her shoulders, her calves, and slipping between her legs. Before she could protest, she was flying again, not as high as she had, but flying all the same, then settling gently back down to see Will's smiling face, close to hers.

'Justine,' he whispered. 'Justine. If you were not already mine, I would have to make you so, after this night. How could I have lived, before I met you? And how could I go on without you?'

'You will not have to,' she whispered. 'I am yours, for now, and for ever.' It was good, for a change, to be speaking the truth to him, for that was what this was. She knew not how, but she would make it so. Diamonds or no diamonds, she would be William Felkirk's wife.

Will stared at the ceiling through half-closed eyes. How good it was to feel this way again, exhausted from lovemaking, half-sleeping, half-waking, with a beautiful woman in his arms. Justine lay curled beside him, sweet and soft as a kitten, her face pressed against his shoulder as if she had fallen asleep in the middle of a kiss.

He was struck, once again, by how unexpected she was. If he'd had to envision the woman he would take as his wife, she would not have been it. He rather thought he'd have ended up with one of the giggling chits at Almack's. Though empty headed, they seemed the most logical choice. He would choose the least annoying of the bunch and marry her. They would be seen around London together, travelling in a smart set, going to parties, dinners, musicals and balls. Eventually, there would be children.

But this girl? Empty headed was the last thing he'd have thought to call her. There was a sense that something was going on, running deep, like the proverbial still waters. But on the surface, there was the quiet of an undisturbed pond. Did she like parties, games and dancing? If so, she did not say.

She liked marmalade and novels. And him. He smiled. In her company, he found an unexpected joy in quiet. The sight of her in his sitting room, in her plain cap, bent over her needlework was a study in contrast. It made him want to uncover the beauty beneath the simple gown and peel back the linen covering her hair, so that he might kiss it.

To find her so willing in his bed, and so bold… He felt another rush of emotion. Desire. Possessiveness. Was it too soon to claim this as love? Had he known her for months, or less than a week?

Or had he known her for ever and spent his life waiting for the moment they might be together? Common sense told him he could not feel love after so short a time in her company. But his heart announced that, in this case, common sense was wrong. There was nothing common about the sensations he felt, when with her. And after tonight, he knew she felt the same when she was with him.

He laid a hand on her hip, smoothing over the curve. As he watched her, she twitched in his arms, went rigid, shuddered, then was still for a moment before going rigid again. Was it a dream? Apparently so, for she did not open her eyes as she tossed her head from side to side as though trying to escape from something or someone. To comfort her, he held her tighter. She jerked away and said, quite plainly, 'Don't touch me. Never again.' Then she sat up, suddenly awake. She gasped for air as though she had been running and looked wildly around her for a moment.

He carefully withdrew his hand from her body. Did his touch frighten her? She had not been bothered by it a few hours before. 'You are safe, Justine. It was only a dream.'

She looked at him for a moment, unable to recognise him. She shrank away from him, wrapping her arms around her body, looking smaller and more helpless than he had seen her.

'It was a dream,' he repeated.

'Only a dream,' she repeated. Then her eyes focused on him and she smiled in relief.

'Do you wish to tell me about it? Sometimes it helps to take away the fear.'

'No!' She shuddered again, then carefully composed herself to show him the usual, placid smile. But it was only an illusion, for her hair still hung damp with sweat on her face and her limbs trembled with suppressed energy.

'Very well,' he said, in a soft calming voice. 'But know that you needn't be afraid, as long as I am here.'

'Of course not,' she said, although she did not sound convinced. Was it nothing more than fantasy? Or was there something in her past that gave her a reason to fear? Life was not always kind to women who were poor and alone. Men could be predatory and a weak girl would not be able to protect herself. Whatever it was, it was clearly no fault of hers, for when he looked at her in the candlelight he could not imagine a more innocent creature. He patted the mattress.' Lay back down beside me. Let me hold you. I will make everything better.'

She did as he bade her, relaxing into his arms as the tension drained from her body. He smoothed her hair away from her face and kissed her temples. 'There, see? Nothing to be afraid of.'

She sighed. 'This feels so good.' She wrapped her arms around him and buried her face in his shoulder again. 'I could sleep here and never wake.'

'Do not say that,' he said, tipping her chin up so he could look in her eyes. 'Do not even think it. Now that I have found you, I do not want to lose you so soon.'

She blinked slowly and, for a moment, he thought that she might be about to cry. But when she spoke, there was no trace of a sob in her voice. 'I am sorry if I frighten you. But in my life, until now, there has not been such happiness. Some of the things in my past, before I met you…were very difficult.'

Difficult. It was said in her quiet, unassuming way, as though she might not truly understand the meaning of the word. Where she might say difficult, another might speak of horror and bear scars greater than the one on his arm that she was now stroking.

Do not touch me? They were the words of someone who had been beaten, or violated. All the more reason for him to be gentle with her and treat her like the treasure she was.

'Are you not the one who taught me it is only the future that matters?' He kissed her again. 'That future will be as sweet as I can make it for you.'

'And for you as well.' She stroked his arm again, running her fingers lightly over the smooth, red patch, where the skin had been ruined by the fire. 'Does it hurt, when I touch you here?'

He shrugged, embarrassed that he could not feel her touch through the thickness of the scar. 'It did at one time. But now I feel nothing.'

'It is the same for me,' she said. 'Sometimes, it is better not to feel anything at all.'

'But you can feel my touch, I hope,' he said sleepily, stroking her arm again.

'Yes,' she said.

'And my scar does not frighten you?' It had been a fearsome thing at one time. Even he had cringed when looking at it.

'I like it,' she whispered back. 'You are like your house. Not too perfect. Just right.'

His throat tightened with a strange rush of emotion, as he remembered her reaction as she had stared up at house and proclaimed it a castle, when most others would have called it a ruin. The touch of her hand on his numb skin made him feel like the battle-scarred king of the keep who had married a princess.

She rolled to face him, her head resting on his damaged shoulder. 'In the dark, when I am by your side, I have but to touch your scar and I will know who you are. I do not even have to open my eyes.'

Strange. 'I am a fortunate man to have a woman love me for my imperfections and not in spite of them.'

His face clouded, for a moment. 'Would you do the same for me, I wonder?'

He smiled back at her, kissing her hair. 'We shall never know, dear. You are perfection. I shall not believe otherwise, no matter what you might say.'

She frowned, as though ready to correct him. So he kissed her once, softly. 'Now, go back to sleep. No more bad dreams.' He touched the tip of her nose with his fingertip.

'Yes, William,' she said with a happy sigh and curled up beside him again, closing her eyes.

Chapter Thirteen

Will rode out to meet his brother that morning, still full of the strangeness of his new life. The horse beneath him was the chestnut gelding. It was a better choice than his foolish attempt to ride Zeus. But while full of spirit, it simply was not Jupiter.

It still hurt to think that he had been the cause of the old horse's death. His father had cautioned him, practically from the cradle, that the Bellston family was known for its hot blood and rash actions. He had taken the advice to heart and been cautious and circumspect in all things. Because of this, his life had been well ordered and scandal-free.

At some point in the last year, his training had failed him. He had lost an old friend and his memory as well. But he'd gained the most precious gift a man could earn: the love of a woman who he could love in return. There was probably something to be learned about the need for balance in all things and the danger of being too punctilious for one's own good, but he could not quite grasp it.

He could remember the feelings of unease, before the christening. He'd had the nagging feeling that his formerly feckless brother was somehow leaving him behind and that his own youth was slipping away unspent. Since then, he had allowed himself to be driven by passion to foolishness.

Not that passion was such a bad thing, when in its rightful place. Most times, Justine was as moderate and sensible as the old William might have wished. But last night, she had proven to be as wild and tempestuous as an adventurous man might have longed for.

They had woken at the dawn and made love again. Her bad dream was forgotten. Each time he'd touched her, she'd laughed. It was a joyous, abandoned sound, as though she'd never laughed before in her life, keeping the happiness bottled inside her until he had come to release it. Her climaxes had been much the same, giddy with desire and overcome with love for him. Her eagerness to please was no longer mechanical and worrisome. It was just her half of a shared gift.

When they were finished, she had thrown herself back into the pillows again, pulling him with her to share kisses and drowse until it was time to rise. When he had left the room for breakfast, she was still there, the covers pulled over her face to reveal nothing but a tangle of red-gold hair. The thought made him smile in a satisfaction deeper than he could ever remember.

Adam cantered up to him on the path leading

away from the house and noticed the change almost immediately. 'Enjoying the summer weather, Will? Or is there some other reason for this total transformation in you?'

'Transformation?'

'Just now, you were grinning like an idiot.'

Will grinned all the harder in response. 'It would be ungentlemanly to say more than that I am a happily married man.'

Adam raised his eyebrows. 'You have rediscovered the reason for your sudden union?'

'Some of it, at least.' If he'd had even a taste of this before they'd married, the need for an immediate elopement was now clear to him. 'Let us say, I am pleased to find her as devoted to me and my happiness as I am to her and hers.'

Adam laughed. 'I would have said something similarly vague after only a short time with Penny. As I remember, you doubted our compatibility.'

'I could not have been more wrong about that,' Will admitted. 'And I am pleased to admit that I have been wrong about Justine. I do not remember what first drew me to her. Perhaps I never will. But I no longer question the rightness of it.' If that much was true, did he really need more? He pushed his previous thoughts aside. 'I think I will not brood over-long about the absence of memory. The present is more than enough to keep me happy.'

'And your wife is settling into her place in your home?'

'She seems to be managing well,' he said. Then added, 'But it will be difficult to know for certain. She really is quite shy. I doubt she would complain if things were difficult.' He thought of her fear in the night, and wondered if he should press her about it. She would deny all, he was sure, and smile until he was convinced that there was no reason to question her.

He gave his brother a worried look. 'She is not likely to request help, even if she needs it. It is as if she does not think herself worthy.'

Adam frowned. 'We noticed similar behaviour when she came to us. I think she is unaccustomed to having family on whom to rely. Perhaps her life was more difficult than she lets on. I am sure, in time, she will come to be more comfortable with you.'

'I should certainly hope so.' Will frowned as well. 'But I should hate to think that I contributed to her isolation in any way. Her sister is some distance from here, boarding in a school in the south.

'You are sending for her, I assume?'

'Of course.' He frowned. 'But why did I part them at all? It was most unkind of me. Justine has no wedding ring on her finger. Did I not bother with that, either?' Nor had he written his family to expect her. 'What if I'd died from this injury, without making provision for her happiness?'

'She arrived with your own ring, worn on a chain around her neck. She said that all was done in a hurry and you had promised to take care of it when you arrived home. In the meanwhile, she has been content to do without and never once complained of it. Do not be so hard on yourself,' Adam finished, with a slight shake of the head. 'A newly married man can be allowed a moment of selfish pleasure.'

So, it had been selfish of him. Even Adam had noticed. And it had been more than a moment. If he understood the situation, he had seduced her without promise of marriage, then kept their union a secret for some weeks. It sounded almost as if he was ashamed of his actions.

Things would change, from this moment on. 'She is always doing without, even when there is no need of it. I will not allow that in the future. I will find some way to bring her out of herself. She is delightful company, when I can get her to speak.'

'So I told you,' Adam said, smiling. 'And she does enjoy her morning stroll.' He pointed ahead of them, on the path. The woman they had been discussing was walking through the wood, pale and quiet as a ghost. She had stopped at the darkest part of the little copse of trees, the dull gold of her gown and spencer blending with the dying leaves. Will had always felt there was a certain air of mystery about it. But today, it was as if they had interrupted a fairy in some mystic rite. 'Justine!' he called. 'What are you doing here, darling?'

Her response to his voice was surprising. Rather than greeting him with pleasure, she started like a

rabbit, turning this way and that, as though searching for concealment. Only when she realised the
hopelessness of escape did she straighten her shoulders and turn to them. She smiled timidly, offering a
curtsy. 'Your Grace. My lor—' She stopped herself
in mid-word and said, 'Will', as though just remembering their relationship.

If Adam thought her behaviour odd, he did not
remark on it. They dismounted and walked their
horses towards her. 'You should have told me that
you wished to visit the grounds,' Will said, being
careful to keep any censure out of his voice. 'We
might have ridden out together.'

'I did not think to, until after you had gone,' she
said, eyes downcast. 'And I prefer to walk.'

'You must find her a horse,' Adam remarked.
'Even for an indifferent rider, the skill can be useful in such remote holdings as ours.'

'You are right, of course,' Will said, thinking of
the placid mare in the stables. He did not wish to see
her cooped up in his house, afraid to ask the servants
to harness the carriage horses. 'If you do not wish
to ride, I will teach you to handle a pony and cart.'
When she looked at him with trepidation, he added,
'Then you might take your sister for rides to the village, whenever you want.'

That was the trick, he suspected. At the mention
of her sister, her mood changed instantly. 'Whenever
I want,' she repeated, with a marvelling smile.

'But today, I hope you are enjoying your morning.' He leaned forward to kiss her lightly on a cheek which was warm with the flush of embarrassment. 'The trees are lovely this time of year, don't you think?'

'It is most glorious,' she agreed.

'The gardens are nice as well. I am surprised to find you here and not touring them.' Nice as it was, this was hardly the most interesting spot on the property.

She paused for a moment, then admitted, 'I was reading something, and it put me in a mood to explore.'

'Really?' He remembered the stack of old books that had been set out in the library and the probable contents of his mother's diary. Then a thought struck him and he smiled. 'Are you chasing ghost stories, my dear? For certainly, if there is a place on the property that is haunted, it must be here, where the murder occurred.'

Perhaps that had not been what she meant. At the mention of death, her face went white as a sheet. 'Here?' she said in a breathless squeak.

'A murder here?' Now it was his brother who was surprised. 'I do not recall any such thing.'

'You were away at school that year,' Will said. 'I was kept home. It was the year I had the fever. Mother told me later that she did not write to you for several months. They were dreadfully worried that, if you guessed how sick I was, you would want to come home and they would lose us all.'

'Ah, yes,' Adam said, remembering. 'You could not have been more than eight at the time.' He looked to Justine, filling in the details of the family history. 'You are lucky to have your husband. I did not learn until much later that he was near death several times that year. We lost our baby sister as well. The details of that will be found in the family Bible, should you be interested.'

'I looked,' she admitted, as though it were some guilty secret. 'But there was no mention of the other man. The murdered one, I mean.' Then she added in a strangely cool voice, 'I should have thought such a thing was worthy of more notice.'

'The household was far too distraught to deal with the situation as it should have,' Will admitted. 'And our mother was an excellent woman, but scatterbrained in such things as record keeping and correspondence. I am not surprised that she did not tell Adam at all.'

'But you knew of it,' she said. 'Even though you were sick.' She was looking from one to the other of them intently. 'I gather the robber was not caught.'

'Robber?' he said. He could not remember if he had mentioned the circumstances.

She glanced around her. 'In a place such as this, the motive must have been robbery.'

'Yes. Of course.' After so much pretended apathy, it was a surprise that such a gruesome tale drew her interest. Or perhaps it was not so surprising. Will had to admit, this particular story was a mystery to him as well. There was something about it, itching and scratching at the back of his mind. Perhaps it was the effort of looking so far into the past that gave him a pain in his head. 'I do not remember many of the details either,' he admitted. 'I heard only bits and pieces of the story myself and was far too sick to care for most of it.' Then he smiled, for he was sure this would interest her. 'But I will tell you one thing that I am sure the family did not write down. I was the one who found the body. I do not remember very clearly.' He glanced at the others in apology. 'That seems to be my excuse for so many things lately. But I was near to lost in the fever, the night the crime occurred. My nurse had fallen asleep and I wandered from bed, looking for something to cool me. The doctor had forbidden that I have ice in my water.' He shook his head, trying to remember. 'I went through the kitchen, down the hill towards the ice house to get some. It is lucky I did not fall into the river and drown myself, for we are very near to it now.'

'And you found a dead man?' Now Justine's eyes were wide with shock.

'Or near dead. I seem to remember him speaking to me.' Will frowned again. 'Although I cannot remember what it was he said. That was probably part of the delirium. He was quite cold when they found him. It took some time for me to get back to the house, and to persuade the family that there was, indeed, something to find here.' He glanced around him, pacing off the space. 'No. Here. Almost exactly. I remember standing beneath this tree and seeing a raven on the branch above me.'

'A raven,' Adam said sceptically.

Will shrugged. 'It was probably another symptom of the fever. The raven screamed and dropped a crown at my feet, then it flew away.' There was that moment of blankness again, where he felt that there was something important that he should remember, but could not.

Then Adam laughed, 'You saw King Arthur? In our wood?'

Will looked to his wife again, who was watching him with round eyes, totally confused. 'Wales is the land of Arthur, my love. If you like fanciful tales, I will read to you of him some night. But there is a legend that he was transformed when he died, and became a raven.'

'Or was buried in a cave. Or taken to Avalon,' Adam supplied unhelpfully. 'There are many stories about what happened to him. But I think we can guess what my little brother was reading, on the night he went wandering in the woods.'

At this, Will laughed himself, then offered up a moment of silence for the poor lost man. 'And here I am, twenty years later, with a head full of nonsense. But that is all I know of the story.

'If you are worried, you needn't be. Adam's lands are quite safe. Even in my father's time, such a crime was the exception, not the rule. This is the only instance I can recall where the perpetrator was not captured and dealt with.'

'You can recall?' she repeated. For a moment, the look of doubt in her eyes was replaced with a sceptical glint.

It was so out of character with her usual passive nature that he laughed. 'We both know how well I can trust my memory. But you can trust me when I tell you that you may walk these paths in safety, day or night, and you will have nothing to fear. Now let me take you up into the saddle and I will give you a ride back to the house, so you do not ruin your slippers in the mud, or misstep and slip down the bank and into the pond. The water on this side is clear as glass and very deep. Perfect for swimming in summer, if you enter on the opposite bank, near Adam's house. But here, it is better for cutting ice. At Christmastime, we will come with skates and you shall see.'

Then he mounted his horse again and scooped his wife up to ride in front of him, so he might point out other, less morbid landmarks of her new home.

Back in her room, Justine glanced down at the mess she had made of her day dress and slippers scuffling around in the leaves of the forest. She had been a fool to go out before ascertaining the location of her husband and the duke. But in his note, Montague had advised that he would meet her near the oak at the head of the village path, should there be news. Until she was sure that Margot was safe, she must at least pretend to obey and make a daily visit to the spot.

Did he know he was directing her to the very place were the murder had occurred? She shivered again. This had been the first morning in ages where her father's death had not been her waking thought. To lie in Will's bed, for even a few minutes, thinking of nothing but the night before was an unimaginable liberty. It could not last, of course. After breakfast, she was back to playing Montague's spy.

She had made her way to the rendezvous point with the hope that she would soon be free of him. Then, out of nowhere, the past had come to remind her of her duty. She must go there again and search more thoroughly.

It had been years, of course. No trace of evidence could have remained. If there were truly diamonds to be discovered, they would not be stuck in a hollow tree where anyone might see them. But she knew she would return to the place, even so. She would not be able to help herself.

It had been even more foolhardy to encourage Will to remember. He might just as well have said, 'Of course. How could I forget Hans be Bryun, the diamond merchant? And you are his daughter, the woman that stood and watched as I was nearly murdered in Bath.' Despite what had happened on the previous evening, she'd have been in custody before she could explain herself.

But she could not have resisted the temptation to ask. It was fortunate that William Felkirk's amnesia was as impervious as ever. Her hopes had risen when he'd admitted to being there the night of the murder. But even then, he could not remember anything helpful. Nothing but useless details about birds and crowns, while her father had lain bleeding in the oak leaves at his feet.

She must remember that he had been but a child and very sick. If there had been a death in the family, and illness, she now knew why the old duke had been far too preoccupied with their own family to give any thought to hers.

But still, to have learned her father's last words after all this time would have been as valuable as diamonds. She let out a sigh and with it she released the last of her bitterness towards the Felkirk family. While her life had been unfair, she must admit that it was no real fault of theirs. Having walked the path where the crime occurred, she had no reason to believe it was not as safe as William claimed. She had always imaged some lawless wilderness where a merchant might fear to tread after dark. But she was sure that there was not so much as a poacher on the land, much less a highwayman. No one could have predicted that his cries for help would be delayed by worries over a sick child. His death was not accidental. But the circumstances around it were much easier to understand then they had been.

It did nothing to ease the hurt of her past. But if

she had thought to get revenge, as Montague had, she could find no logical justification for it. The duke, his wife and her William were quite blameless in what had happened to her father, and to her.

But if they were not at fault, then who was? If the path was not particularly dangerous, how had someone discovered her father on it? He would not have announced, when passing through the local inn, that he carried a bag of valuable stones in his pocket. Yet, someone must have known of his plans and waited on the path for him.

'I have something for you.'

She started again and looked up to see Will standing in the doorway that connected their bedrooms. She must learn not to jump at the sound of her husband's voice. It should be as familiar to her as her own. And after last night, sleeping in his arms, she had to admit that it was a pleasure to hear. At the memory, she remembered to greet him with a smile. 'A gift? I am sure, whatever it is…'

'Is not necessary? On the contrary, the thing I bring is yours already. You should have had it for some time. Giving it to you was one more thing that I had forgotten.' He held out a closed fist to her. 'Close your eyes and open your hand.'

She did as he wished, trying to stifle the feeling of excitement. He might be simply be rewarding her for her behaviour in bed with him. She had received such gifts before and felt the disappointment and shame that came with them. Could not the pleasure be enough to satisfy them both?

Then, she felt the slim, cool band of metal resting on her palm. She had an illogical desire to yank her hand away before she opened her eyes and saw what she knew must lie there.

'I must have promised you this, I am sure,' Will said, in the voice he used when trying to manufacture memories to fill the void of the last six months. 'It belonged to my mother and was set aside, waiting for my marriage.' He shuffled his feet, as though embarrassed that he could not offer her more. 'It is not so grand as the duchess ring, of course. Although I doubt Penny would mind giving it up to you, should you want it. She says it is far too heavy to be practical. All of the best pieces are already in her jewel box. But they are entailed. This is mine. And now, it is yours.'

He withdrew his hand to show the delicate gold setting with a single rose-cut diamond at the centre of it. She could not help her instincts. What her father had not bred into her, Montague had taught, so that she might be his partner in the shop. She held the stone up to the light, searching for flaws.

It did not shine as a brilliant cut might, but the stone was perfect, a testament to elegance. The setting was etched with vines and made it look even more like the flower it was meant to represent. The colour was a clear blue-white, the weight, if she subtracted the gold, was slightly over a carat.

It was not worth as much as the stones her father had lost. But should she sell it, she would have several thousand pounds. It was more than enough to launch both herself and her sister on a new life, free of the interference of Mr Montague.

'Don't you like it?' Will was still standing before her, hand outstretched, ready to place it on her finger. Instead of responding with gratitude, she was calculating the value of a lover's gift.

She closed her eyes for a moment. When she opened them, she spoke from her heart. 'It does not matter to me what Penny has. This is the most beautiful ring I have ever seen. I would not trade it for the world.'

'That is what I hoped to hear,' Will said, with a satisfied smile.

It was true. She wanted this ring as she had no other. She'd no jewellery of her own, other than the string of pearls she had been given on her sixteenth birthday. They had been her mother's and had been less a present than an inheritance. For all the other pieces that passed through her hands, she had never been more than a model. A pretty neck to hang things on so that Montague might sell them. She had long since stopped coveting them.

The more she looked at this ring, the more she wanted it and all it symbolised. She burned to have it and to have the man that held it. It meant safety, peace and an unbroken circle of union.

'Let me help you.' He meant with the ring, of course. He wanted to put it on her finger. But something in his voice was coaxing her to tell him how much help she really needed.

She let herself be wooed and closed her eyes again. He slipped it on and whispered, 'With this ring, I thee wed. With my body, I thee worship. With all my worldly goods I thee endow.' Then he warmed the finger with a kiss. She opened her eyes to see him looking up into hers. 'That is right, isn't it? Were they the words I spoke to you, when we married?'

She did not know, nor did she care. They were the words he'd spoken to her, right at this instant, and she could feel that he meant them. 'They are perfect,' she whispered back.

As was the ring. The fit was comfortable. The weight was not awkward. It added elegance to the hand. It made her want to gesture, casually, so that others might notice and envy what her husband had given to her. She could not stop looking at it. And she could not stop smiling.

He gave a sigh of relief. 'You do like it. Sometimes, I wonder. You are so quiet and too easily pleased. I cannot always tell your mood. As I have told you before, you must not do things just to please me.'

'Of course I like it,' she said. 'And...' She stopped, frozen. Then she said what she was thinking. 'And I love the man who has given it to me.' Unlike so many other things she said, it was truth. An inconvenient truth, perhaps. She still did not know how to free herself from Montague, or what might happen if Will remembered Bath. But even if there could be no future for them, she had to share her feelings.

Things were not as bad as she feared. Or perhaps they were worse. He wanted to help her. Soon, she would ask him for aid and see if he was as good as his word. If she truly loved him, she would have to tell him the truth. But not today. The moment was too perfect to risk ruining it with talking.

So she threw her arms around his neck and kissed him. This was truth as well. She liked kissing him. She liked being kissed by him. She liked the way it felt to touch him and to have him touch her.

'You love me,' he said, when their lips had parted. It would have been better had he declared his feelings for her. It was unfair of her to expect that. No matter what she had been telling him, he had known her but a few days.

But she had been watching over him for weeks, and in that time she had found nothing that was not admirable. She knew him now, better than she knew herself. Though it was not real, it was just the sort of marriage she could have wished for. 'I love you,' she repeated. 'And, if you are not too busy, or too tired, I should like to go to your room now.' She smiled into his chest, letting her ringed finger play with the buttons on his waistcoat.

He laughed. 'I cannot imagine a better response to this gift, or a better way to celebrate it.' He kissed the top of her head. 'In the days before the accident, did I tell you what a delight you are, my beautiful Justine?'

'I do not recall,' she said. 'But you might say it all again, if it is true.'

'Later,' he said. 'At the moment, I have a much more physical demonstration of my feelings.'

Chapter Fourteen

It was nearly a week since they had moved to the old manor and life could not have been better. Justine had grown so used to behaving as a wife to Will that it no longer felt like play acting. She loved the shared meals and the quiet evenings with lacework and novels. She especially loved what happened after, when she retired to her husband's room. Even if they did nothing more than sleep in each other's arms, there was a warmth more cosy than the fire in the drawing room and a peace stronger than she'd ever known.

All the same, Justine tempered her excitement at the arrival of her sister with a very real fear. Suppose Mr Montague learned of her plan and put a stop to it? She had been able to avoid him thus far. Three days' steady rain had made walks in the woods impossible. She had persuaded Will to send a carriage to meet the coach in Cardiff, thus avoiding a chance meeting between Margot and their guardian at the local inn. But there were still so many things that might go wrong.

Suppose, once she arrived, Margot blurted out the truth, or asked embarrassing questions that could not be answered. She had shielded the poor girl from her sordid relationship with their guardian. Margot thought of him as nothing more than a rather silly older man. As such, she did not know why she needed protection. There was nothing more dangerous than not knowing of the risk.

Now that the day of Margot's arrival had come, Justine was pacing the floor of the morning room, staring out the window for the approaching carriage. 'You need not worry,' Will said, taking her hands in his and kissing them. 'I have persuaded Adam to send the barouche. The ride will be comfortable and the driver will take utmost care.'

Justine smiled at the thought. Margot must have started in disbelief at the sight of the Bellston crest on the door and the liveried servants calling her Miss de Bryun with a bow, eager to be of service. Even if it was only an illusion, it would be a memory that she could share with her children, should she have any. The chances she might marry and have those children would increase once she was safely out of the clutches of Montague.

At last, she heard the distant jingle of harnesses through the open window, and the approach of the carriage, the calls of the coachman and the butler at the door, ready to welcome the new guest. She hurried to the hall and pushed past him so she could be at the foot of the carriage steps when her sister alighted.

For a moment, Margot was framed in the open door of the carriage above her. Then she took the few steps to the ground as if in a daze, staring up at the house in front of her. Before she could say a word, Justine rushed forward and enfolded her in her arms.

For a moment, she forgot everything but how good it was to see Margot again. It had been too long since they had been together and even longer since they had been able to speak freely. Before they could do that, it would be longer still. But for now, it felt as if their troubles were over. She whispered in hurried French in the girl's ear, 'Guard your tongue, Margot. The situation is complicated. I will explain everything soon. For now, all you must know is that I am Lord Felkirk's wife and this is my home.'

'For now?' Her sister whispered the two words back, then let it pass, allowing Justine to take her arm and lead her into the house. She stared up at the high ceiling and wide stone stairs that had been part of the original castle. 'Your home? *C'est magnifique.*'

'It is,' agreed Justine, in a whisper.

'It is your home as well, my dear.' William had arrived in the hall in just in time to hear the compliment to the house he held so dear. He stepped forward to offer his hand to her. 'Introductions are in order, I think.' He looked expectantly at Justine and flashed a disarming smile to show that his formality was little more than a jest.

It gave her a strange thrill of pride to see Margot's reaction to her dear William. At his worst, when he'd been wasting away in the sickbed, Justine had thought him tragically handsome. But today, he must have requested Stewart to take extra care with his dressing so that he might make a good impression on their guest. He was turned out in a coat of midnight-blue superfine and the snowy-white cravat made his hair look as dark as a raven's wing in comparison. The walking stick he had chosen was not the common wood staff he'd been using around the house, but ebony chased with silver and topped with a polished ivory knob. She was sure that she had never seen him look better. In fact, she doubted there was a more handsome man in all of London. And by the dazzled look in Margot's eyes, her sister thought the same. 'Lord William Felkirk, may I present my sister, Miss Margot de Bryun,' she said, smiling back at him.

Will made a very proper bow in response to Margot's awed curtsy. Then he gestured into the house. 'No need to linger in the doorway, my dear. Come in and be comfortable. Would you care for refreshment? Are you in need of rest? There is a room prepared for you. There will be one in our London home as well. Once you are settled, we will send for the rest of your things.'

'My things?' Apparently, it had not occurred to her that the visit might be permanent. 'I must go back to school,' she said to Justine in a half-whisper. 'Mr—'

Justine rushed to cut off mention of their guardian and his wishes on the matter. 'Now that I am married, I would prefer that you stayed here with us.'

'At the very least, you must consider a school nearer to us,' Will added. 'Your sister pines for you, when you are not nearby. And I would not see her unhappy, even for a moment.' Then he gave his most winning smile, using his good looks to charm the girl into agreement.

It appeared he had made a conquest, for Margot's eyes widened in surprise, and gave a confused nod of assent, Mr Montague all but forgotten. 'You are too kind, my lord.'

'William, please,' he said. 'Or Will. You are my family now, just as Justine is. She will show you your room and give you a tour of the house. Then, perhaps, we shall have tea in the garden. Tonight we will dine with the duke and duchess, who are most eager to meet you.'

Justine needn't have worried about the girl blurting secrets. Margot was already stunned nearly to silence. But the casual announcement that they would be dining with a peer reduced her to mute shock.

'Come, Margot,' Justine said, tugging on her hand to propel her towards the stairs. 'Let me show you to your room. We have much to talk about, for it has been ages since last we saw each other.'

'We certainly do,' Margot agreed, staring back over her shoulder at her new brother-in-law, as they mounted the stairs.

Once they were alone in her room, Margot sat down on the bed, giving one satisfied bounce on the soft mattress before looking at her with curiosity, waiting for her to speak.

Justine sank down beside her, unsure of where to begin.

Margot held out her hands as though expecting the explanation to drop into them. 'Do you mean to tell me the meaning of this, or do you leave me to guess? And do not think you can lie to me over this, Justine. At least not any more than you already have.'

Justine recoiled in shock from the accusation. 'When have I ever lied to you?'

'When have you ever told me the truth?' Margot answered. 'You hardly speak to me at all, if speaking is what I can call the sparse letters you send to me in Canterbury.'

'The shop has been busy,' she said, trying to evade the truth. 'There has not been time to write much.'

'If it is busy, then I should be there with you, helping,' Margot replied. 'And then we might speak whenever we wished.'

'A shop is no place for an impressionable young woman,' Justine said firmly.

Margot scoffed. 'It is a jewellery shop, not an alehouse. And you have been working in it since you were two years younger than I am now.'

Justine felt a moment's revulsion at the true nature of her duties. At seventeen, she had been more naïve than Margot was now, and fallen easily into the trap Montague had set for her. Then repeated what she said each time Margot argued for a return to Bath. 'Perhaps, when you have completed your education...'

'I have more than enough education to take my place in a family business,' her sister said. 'I am older than most of the girls at the school and have learned all that they can teach me. Everyone remarks on the way I remain there between terms, as if I have no family at all.' The girl's face clouded and she appeared on the verge of tears. 'Whatever I have done to earn this rejection from you, I am sorry for it. I will prove I have learned my lesson, if you will but let me come home.'

'Do not think that,' Justine said hurriedly, putting an arm around the girl. 'It is nothing you have done. I have done what I have done to protect you.'

'But why do I need protection? Why must I remain in school, so far away from you? Can you not at least tell me that?'

At this, she hugged Margot close and felt tears wetting the shoulder of her gown. She had hidden so much, in an attempt to keep her sister pure. What could she reveal now that would calm her fears? 'Do not cry, little one. Our separation is at an end. You will live here, now, with Lord Felkirk and myself. It was never my desire that we be apart. The situation in Bath was...complicated.'

Margot lifted her head and rolled her eyes. 'If this is over you and Mr Montague, I know of it already.'

Justine shrank back, horrified.

Margot smiled at her. 'I have seen the way he looks at you, Justine. And I have seen him kiss you, when you both think I am not nearby.'

'You know?' She could not understand the whole truth, or she would not speak so casually of her sister's disgrace.

'Of course. It is quite plain that he has a *tendre* for you. He must wish to wed you, even though that is not at all proper for a guardian.' She frowned. 'Since you have been of age for years, and I have heard no announcement of engagement, I assumed that you were not similarly interested. But that does not explain why you married another so suddenly. And why did you not tell me of it immediately?' Margot's tears had dried. But it was clear that she was still deeply hurt by the sudden turn of fortune.

Justine smoothed her sister's hair and kissed her lightly on the cheek. 'I am sorry I did not tell you immediately. But my dear, the situation is so much more complicated than you think.'

The ever-pragmatic Margot pulled away and cocked her head to the side, as though considering. 'I fail to see why. I assume you kept me in the dark because you have not told Mr Montague of the marriage. Since you are of age already, you can do what you wish without his permission. Do not mind his tender heart, if your happiness lies with another. Simply demand your inheritance and go. If you wish, I will return to Bath and explain for you.'

'No,' Justine said hurriedly. 'You must not. I have not told you before because I am not actually married to Will.'

Margot's jaw dropped. 'You are his mistress?'

'No. That is not it either.' And how was she to explain the rest of it? 'There was an accident,' she said. 'Lord Felkirk was injured and I was responsible. He remembers nothing of our meeting, or what happened after. I brought him here and told his family we were married.'

At this, Margot laughed. 'How did you come to meet the man in the first place, much less cause an accident?'

'This next will be difficult to explain. When Father died…' Justine took her sister's hand '…he was here, Margot. On the road that runs just past this house. Lord Felkirk was the one who found him. He sought me out in Bath, claiming that he found the diamonds. But then…there was an accident.'

Margot withdrew her hand. 'And you are only pretending to be married to him so that you can find the stones.'

'They are ours, Margot. We have but to find them. If we sell them, we shall have more than enough money to last a lifetime. We need not go back to Bath at all.'

The girl looked more disappointed by this revelation than she had at any of the others. 'We have more than enough money now, Justine. Is not half the jewellery shop rightly ours?'

'Well, yes,' she admitted. 'But it is not the same as money in the purse. Mr Montague—'

'Mr Montague has managed both halves for years,' Margot interrupted. 'As long as it is profitable, I see no reason he cannot continue to do so. You may not approve of it, dear sister, but when I am old enough, I mean to help him there. You might tell me that it is improper to do so, but I know just as much about gems as you and am ever so much better at maths than I am at lacemaking.'

It was a future that Justine had not bothered to imagine. Once Margot was safely of age, Montague might cease to threaten the girl's innocence and allow her to marry. But if she insisted on returning to her old home, she would be walking into a trap. The only way to escape him would be to sell the business and start again.

'If Father knew what had become of us, he would not wish us to remain in partnership with Mr Montague,' she said, as gently as possible. 'He would want us to find the diamonds and take them as our real inheritance. Or perhaps appeal to the Duke of Bellston for help. If he wished you to continue in business, Father would rather have seen you with a shop of your own than beholden to Mr Montague.'

Her sister sighed and took her hand. 'Justine, it has been twenty years. You still talk of finding justice for Father and regaining what was once ours. It has earned you nothing but trouble. This wild scheme of pretending to be Lord Felkirk's wife is proof of that.'

'I had my reasons,' Justine said, trying not to let her frustration show.

Margot shook her head. 'I cannot understand what they could possibly be. But I know you must let go of this quest for lost family treasure. Perhaps it is because you can remember Father and our old life in Belgium. But I cannot. He was dead before I was born, Justine. Mother died when I was still young. I have known nothing but England and school, and Mr Montague. And difficult though he is, he is not such a bad man.'

'He is evil, Margot,' Justine said, unable to contain the truth. 'I cannot go back to him. And I will not allow you to do so, either.'

'I fail to see how you can stop me,' Margot said, in a reasonable tone. 'In a year, I will be old enough to make my own decisions on the matter. My own mistakes as well.' She gave her sister an arch look. 'But whatever I do, I suspect it will not end with me in a false marriage to a stranger. How you can manage to stay out of the man's bed is beyond me.' She paused and then said in a worried voice, 'Lord Felkirk is a most handsome man, of course. And kind as well. But I trust that you have not stooped so low as to give up your honour to convince him that you are his wife. If Mother were alive, she'd have told you that virtue is more precious than the diamonds you are searching for.'

'Lord Felkirk has been ill. He is still very weak.' Hopefully, this was enough of an answer to set Margot's suspicions to rest. But it left Justine sickened by her own lies.

'Good,' her sister said with a relieved sigh. 'I would not want to know if you thought so little of yourself that you would seek a man's protection for expediency's sake. All the same, it is obvious that the man dotes on you. Tell him the truth as quickly as possible. It is likely he will forgive all and marry you, then you will have nothing to worry about.' She smiled and added, 'Only then will I come to live with you, at least until I am of age. It is much nicer here than at school.' She gave another little bounce on the mattress and ran her hand over the painted silk of the coverlet.

'I will do as you wish, when I am able,' Justine said, with a sigh. 'But it is not time for the whole truth. At least, not just yet. Until then, you must keep my secret. Can you do that?'

Margot sighed and fell back on to the bed, staring up at the ceiling, as though she'd had quite enough of her sister, her worries and her complicated problems. 'Of course I will. But do not wait too long, sister. For Lord Felkirk's sake, you must be honest.'

That night, a dinner was held to honour the visitor at the duke's manor. If Margot had been impressed by the luxury of Will's house, she was truly dazzled by an invitation from the handsome duke and his plainspoken, bespectacled duchess. Justine hoped that they were not imposing in some way. Bellston was quiet this evening, offering a warm greeting to his brother and a somewhat more reserved welcome to both Margot and Justine.

But Penny was as gracious and affectionate as ever, anxious to make Miss de Bryun feel welcome. She complimented her on her education, quizzing her in Greek and Latin, and declaring her quite proficient for a girl of such few years.

At this, Daphne Colton rolled her eyes. 'Such skills will leave you permanently on the shelf, if you display them in London, Miss de Bryun. But since you are as perfect as your sister, we will take care not to let that happen.' She reached down the table to touch the girl's cheek and turning her head from side to side, admiring her profile. 'If you were turned out in the latest fashion, there would be none to compare to you. We must take you shopping.'

Penny laughed. 'Even I know that there are no suitable shops within miles of here.'

'There are in London,' Daphne said. 'It is quiet there, now. But surely Bond Street would welcome commerce.' She glanced at Justine. 'Have plans been made for a Season for her? She is very nearly of age, is she not? It is rather old to be making a come out, but if she is sponsored by a duchess, I should not think it too late. Now that Will is doing so much better, we might all go south for a week or two.'

Margot shot a surprised look in her direction, unsure how to respond to such a generous offer.

London was the last place Justine wanted to be.

It would be dangerous to call attention to the fact that Margot was not in Canterbury, as Montague expected her to be. 'I do not think that would be possible. The expense...'

Daphne gave a wave of her hand. 'It is miniscule, compared to what she will gain by a good marriage. Will has the blunt for it, I am sure. It would be a shame for such a pretty girl to remain a spinster, don't you think, Penn?'

'I do not think we are entitled to an opinion on the matter, without speaking to Miss de Bryun,' the duchess said with a smile, turning to the girl. 'Perhaps she has more important goals.'

Margot blinked, still surprised that the conversation had turned to her. 'I do not think I should mind being married,' she said cautiously, 'if the gentleman is as kind as Lord Felkirk.' She shot a quick glance at her sister that made Justine feel, had she been close enough to reach, she would have received a sisterly kick on the shin. 'But my plan for some time has been to manage a jewellery shop.'

Justine stopped her fork, halfway to her mouth. Of all the subjects she had warned Margot to avoid, had she remembered that this one was most important?

'Sometimes, I think my wife would like that as well,' Tim Colton replied with a sigh. 'She would have me buy out the jewellers, on each trip to town. What she means to do with it all, I am not sure. She has but one neck, after all.'

Margot opened her mouth, ready to correct the

misunderstanding. But before she could say more, Daphne let out a short, merry laugh. 'Then we must make sure that your husband is both kind and willing to spoil you as mine does.'

As she spoke, Justine at last caught her sister's eyes, and gave her a desperate look that warned her to silence. Then she gave a flourish of her own hand, to indicate the ring Will had given her. 'A single, perfect gift is more than enough to please me.' She gave a nod to her smiling husband and accepted the approving comments of the ladies at the table that it was, indeed, a most lovely ring.

Only the duke was silent, his eyes speculative, his lips set in a straight, inflexible line.

It was nearly midnight when Will called for the carriage. He'd have been happy to stay some hours more, partnering his sister-in-law at whist, while Justine sat in the corner with Penny and her lacework. But it was clear that Miss de Bryun was close to dozing over her cards, probably tired from the long journey to Wales.

When he went into the hall to find the butler, his brother followed him. The duke's steps on the marble tile were sharp, almost military in cadence as he hurried to catch him. 'A moment, Will. I need a word before you go.'

Will turned and waited. His brother had been behaving strangely all evening. Perhaps now he would learn the reason for it.

Adam glanced back at the open door to the salon where Justine and her sister were taking leave of their hostess. Then he said, *sotto voce*, 'There has been a discovery that concerns the time you were missing from us. Tomorrow I will come for you, in the carriage. Tell any who ask…' He paused as though searching his mind for a likely lie. 'Tell them we are going to purchase a horse. But until tomorrow, be cautious.'

'In what way?' What risk could there be in a short ride to his own home and a night in bed?

The ladies were coming into the hall to join them and Adam gave no answer but a warning shake of his head. Then he turned to his guests. To an outsider, there would be nothing unusual in his behaviour. His Grace, the Duke of Bellston, was ever a genial host.

But Will had known him for a lifetime and recognised the mood for what it was. Adam was playing a role, just as he did when playing politics in London. His true feelings, whatever they might be, were buried so deep that Will would not know them until the morning.

Chapter Fifteen

'Are you going to explain the purpose of this trip? Or do you mean to leave me guessing?'

Will's question was met by silence from his brother, who sat in the opposite seat of the coach, staring out of the window as though he had not heard.

After Adam's warning, Will had half-expected that there would be an attack on his person as he rode home. But the remainder of the night had been uneventful. Young Margot had chattered all the way home, amazed at the manor, the food and the hospitality of the duke and duchess.

Justine had smiled behind her hand and did her best to calm the girl, assuring her that she had made an excellent impression on them. Once they had sent their guest off to bed, they had gone to bed themselves. And once again, Justine proved what a lucky man he was, to have married so well.

Will smiled at his brother and waved a hand before his face to get his attention. 'You said this was about my lack of memory. If you are carting me off to prison for something, the least you could have done is let me say a proper goodbye to my wife.'

Adam shook his head. 'It was nothing you did. At least, I do not think so.'

'What the devil does that mean?' Other than that the situation had changed from annoying to alarming.

'It means that I do not know what to say, until I have seen for myself the thing that Jenks described to me and your reaction to it. If we are wrong, as I pray we are, then it will be better that I had not spoken at all.'

'Very well, then.' Will gave an expansive gesture. 'Continue to be mysterious. But you might at least tell me where we are going.' They had been on the road for nearly an hour and he was beginning to fear that the whole of the day would be wasted.

'It is not much longer,' his brother allowed. 'There is an inn a little up the way. The Fox and Hare. We do not stop there often. The ale is watered and the food is mediocre at best. But yesterday, while transporting Miss de Bryun, there was some problem with a carriage wheel and a stop needed to be made. Jenks saw something of interest in the stables and wished our opinion of it.'

'You want me to see a horse?' he said. He'd thought last night's comment had been nothing more than a ruse. 'I do not wish to buy one, if that is what you have been told. I am not ready to make such a purchase today, at any rate.'

Adam shook his head again. 'This horse will interest you, I think. But we must go see for ourselves.'

They pulled into the coach yard a short time later and followed Jenks and the driver directly to the place where the horses were kept. The coachman was shifting uneasily, foot to foot. 'I thought you would want to know, my lord. I am sure you will think it foolish of us and see the obvious difference.'

'There is no difference,' Jenks said flatly. 'It is what we think it is. But only Lord Felkirk can tell us so.'

'Can tell you what?' Will said, his patience growing thin. 'I still have no idea what you are on about.'

From a stall halfway down the row there came the thump of hooves hitting boards.

'Careful with that one,' a stable boy called. 'We can barely handle him.'

'I am sure we are up to the task,' Will said, taking a firmer grip on his stick.

They were standing in front of the animal in question now. At the sound of his voice, there came a frantic whinny.

He knew that sound.

It was impossible. But he could not doubt his own ears. He pushed past the stable boy, dropped his stick and put a hand on the neck of the horse, reaching for his tossing head.

'Now tell them they are fools and that all black horses look alike.' His brother's voice had a plaintive quality to it, as though wishing could give him the answer he wanted.

But to say that would have been foolish. All black horses did not look the same, any more than all blonde women looked like Justine. This black horse looked exactly like Jupiter, because it was Jupiter. He ran a hand on over the horse's shoulder and felt the height, just as he remembered it.

The spirited horse calmed instantly. It was not because he had any gift for animals, but because the horse recognised his touch, just as it had known his voice.

'Hello, old fellow. It has been some time, has it not? Did you miss me?' He turned the face so that he might look into the eyes and the gigantic head gave a nod as if to say, 'Yes.'

Will stroked the soft, black nose and got another nod of approval and a nudge at his pocket, where the sugar should be.

This was impossible. Many men kept a treat of some kind in their pinks. This was no indication of recognition, just a learned behaviour. As for the rest, he was only seeing what he wished to see and hearing what he wished to hear. It could not be Jupe. Jupiter had died because of the same fall that injured him.

Will walked to the back of the stall, trailing his hands along the smooth back. There was the barely noticeable pattern of white hairs on the flank. He felt under them and found the fine line of the scar from the time they had taken a fall, going over a fence in a hunt. How he had worried over that, walking the young horse home, and fussing over him until the scratch had healed. But there should be other scars, should there not?

Perhaps Justine had been misled about the extent of the injury. The fall in Bath that had laid him low must have done some damage to the horse. He stroked down the back, the withers and the legs, all the way to the hooves, and could find none. Jupe was as sound as the day he'd ridden out on his way to Bath, to see Mr Montague.

Montague.

The scrap of memory appeared, as though it had always been there. He had found the bag in his nursery dresser, searching for a gift for Billy. Just a scrap of silk and velvet that he'd used to hold pretty rocks. But more properly, it was meant to hold loose stones. A jeweller's bag. And where had he got it?

In the woods.

He gripped Jupe's neck, now, letting the horse support him as he searched his mind for the rest of the story.

'My lord?' Jenks was leaning close now, fearing that his behaviour was a sign of weakness.

Will waved him away. Standing on his own feet again. 'You were right. This is Jupiter.'

'You know what this means, don't you?' Adam was speaking now and his voice was surprisingly bitter.

How was he to answer? Did he know what it meant? In truth, he did not. More than Adam knew, perhaps. He knew the facts. He had found a jeweler's bag in the nursery and pieced together the story of the murder by questioning the oldest servants. A diamond merchant had died and the stones had been stolen. No one could remember more than that.

He had traced the origin of the bag through the monogram on the silk: the entwined M and B of Montague and de Bryun set in an embroidered gold crown. He had gone to Bath, seeking information about the bag's missing contents.

The woman in the main salon of the store had been too beautiful to be an ordinary shop girl. Her satin gown was too bright for day, and too low, revealing a pale throat hung with emeralds. Her hair swept high on her head, to show ears hung with matching drops. Her fingers were heavy with rings, her wrists circled with bracelets. It was as if a statue had been decorated and come to life as a walking advertisement for the store.

Her face had been just as impassive as a statue's as well. In her eyes, he had seen far too much knowledge for one so young. The smile she wore was too polite and distant to be anything but ironic.

Montague had come into the room and looked at her, eyes flicking from gem to gem as though counting his possessions. The final intimate sweep of his eyes indicated that his ownership did not end with the jewellery she wore. When he turned to look at

Will, there was a faint warning in his expression. One might look at the merchandise, and the woman beneath it, but one must never touch.

And then, to Will's shock, he had introduced her as de Bryun's own daughter.

Montague himself had been strangely familiar. He had seen the face before, he was sure of it. But he could not think where. The man had escorted him into a parlour at the back of the shop, where they might talk in private. But he had quickly become irrational over what were simple and innocent questions.

It was clear that Will would learn nothing more than what he already knew. As he turned to go, he saw the woman, standing before him, blocking the door.

And then, pain. The last thing he could remember, before darkness closed over him was those knowing green eyes.

He knew what had happened. But that still did not explain how it had come to this.

'I said, do you know what this means?' Adam was shaking his shoulder. 'She lied to us, Will. I took her into my home. I treated her as family. I encouraged you to trust her.'

If he'd not still been in shock himself, he'd have found it funny. The Duke of Bellston was ranting over his injured dignity and abused hospitality. As if that was worse than surviving a murder attempt, only to fall in love with one of your attackers. How she must have laughed, to find him so easily manipulated.

'Who knows if there is any truth at all in what she said? But fear not. I will call out the watch and we will take her into custody immediately. Then we shall have the real story out of her. Her sister as well. The girl is likely an accomplice to whatever happened.'

'You will not.' At last he had found his voice. With a final pat, he turned away from the horse and silenced his brother with a look. 'You will get in the carriage, ride home and say nothing to anyone.' Then he looked at Jenks. 'Find out what you can of the man who left the horse. If he is still here, set someone to watch him. Follow him, if necessary. But do nothing until I give you direction.'

'And what do you mean to do, while this is going on?' Adam was still angry and using a warning tone to remind him that a man who was both a peer and one's older brother should be given the respect he had earned.

'I mean to saddle my horse and ride home.' He held up a hand to silence objections. 'And I will tolerate no nonsense about my being too weak to ride. It is not as if I am likely to fall off of Jupiter, now is it?'

His sarcasm shocked the two other men to silence. But the horse answered with a soft nicker of amusement.

He turned back to Jupiter, stroking his face. 'Do not laugh at me. I thought you dead. I grieved over your loss. And all the while you were eating oats and snapping at stable boys.' He looked up to see the other two, still staring at him, as though trying to decide if his current behaviour was a sign that the recent injury had driven him mad.

'Go,' he said, more softly to his brother. 'Please, keep what you have learned to yourself for a time. A day or two, at most. I need time to think. And to speak with…Justine.'

He had almost said *my wife*. And what a bitter lie that was. He put it aside and continued. 'I will send word when I have decided how best to proceed. You needn't worry. Now that I am aware of the situation, there is no risk.'

No risk at all, now that he knew not to turn his back on Justine de Bryun or her lover.

Chapter Sixteen

'I don't know why you bother attempting to teach me this,' Margot said, looking at the mass of knots that was her first attempt at lacemaking. 'Of all the skills I might wish to develop to honour our family, this is not one of them.'

Justine bit her lip in frustration. Margot was still talking of the shop and her desire to return to Bath as soon as Mr Montague allowed it. While her younger sister might deny any allegiance to a father she had never met, she seemed to have inherited that man's business acumen. 'It is better that you cultivate virtues that might attract a husband. With Lady Colton's offer of a Season and the sponsorship of the Duchess of Bellston...'

Margot laughed. 'It is a lovely dream, of course. But no gentleman will want to marry the daughter of a merchant.'

'You would also be a member of the Felkirk family,' Justine reminded her.

Her sister responded with a surprised look. 'You know that I am not. Have you forgotten what you told me, just yesterday? You are not truly married to Lord Felkirk.'

For a moment, she had forgotten. The truth was becoming increasingly clouded by what happened each night, when she was alone with Will. Today, all she could remember was the sweet kiss he had given her in parting. Then he had gone off with his brother in the carriage, saying something about the possibility of purchasing a horse.

That would be good for him, she was sure. He still pined for the one he had lost. While no other animal was likely to take the place of Jupiter, it was better that certain, unexplainable parts of his past be put aside.

She was thinking like a wife, again. It left her unsure whether to smile or frown. If love were all that was necessary to make a marriage, she would be his true wife. 'For the moment, you are right,' she admitted to Margot. 'I am not Will's wife. But you were also right when you said that I must find a way to explain to him. For I do so wish…' She bit her lip again. She wished that their meeting had occurred, just as she had imagined it. For how could she ever tell him the truth?

'You love him?' Margot said, softly.

'Very much,' Justine admitted. 'I cannot imagine life without him. And I am so afraid, when he learns what I have done…'

Her sister rose and put an arm about her shoulders. 'Do not distress yourself. I am sure you will find a way through this. Once you have told him the truth, he will forgive you for the ruse and all will be well again.'

'You cannot know that,' Justine said.

'Nonsense. It is clear that he adores you,' Margot said. 'But it will not change my opinion on the matter of a marriage for myself, or my plans for the future. With you married and living here, someone must go back to Bath and be the second half of Montague and de Bryun.'

'That will not be possible,' Justine said, in a tone she hoped would brook no argument. After all she had sacrificed to keep the girl safe, she seemed intent on throwing herself from the frying pan into the fire.

'Sometimes, I think you are simply jealous of my interest,' Margot said. 'If you did not enjoy your place there, it was unfair of you to exile me, so that you need not share our birthright.'

Justine set her lace aside and turned to take her sister's hand. 'It is not from jealousy that I keep you away. I do not want the place that I have, Margot. I would be quite happy if I were never to see Mr Montague or that horrible store again. If you were to know the whole of it, you would not want it either.'

'Then tell me the whole of it, and let me decide.'

For a moment, she was tempted to tell all. What would it feel like, to finally be free of the worst secrets of her life in Bath? Then, silently, she shook her head.

Margot gave a short, frustrated sigh, glanced out the window and smiled. 'Then perhaps I shall ask Mr Montague what problem lies between you. I believe that is him coming up the drive right now.'

Justine had not thought of this possibility, when she had ceased going to the wood to wait for him. The last three days, there had been letters from Mr Smith in the morning post. She had thrown them away unopened, not wanting to read the demands for information, and the threats of punishment for disobedience. Once Margot was safe with her, what could the man do? She was sure he would not dare to come to the house and risk being seen by Will.

But Will was gone, travelling in a carriage past the very spot that Montague would have waited for her. He knew she was alone and unprotected. Thus, he had come to the house, knowing that she could not avoid him without raising suspicions.

'Margot, go to your room.' At the very least, she could prevent him from seeing or threatening her sister.

She had not counted on her sister having an opinion. 'Certainly not,' Margot said, settling herself in her chair to prove she had no intention of moving.

'It is not wise that you remain,' Justine said, firm but gentle. 'We did not get his permission for this trip. It is quite likely he will be angry.'

'Angry at you, more likely,' Margot answered

with a wicked smile. 'Your crimes are far worse than mine, misleading this poor family and luring me away from school.'

'It is not that way at all,' Justine said, in a desperate whisper. The enemy was so close he might hear their argument through the half-open window of the morning room.

Margot gestured towards that same window. 'It is he who deserves the explanation, not me. Since you have been trying to dissuade me from my goals all morning, I am not in a mood to help you out of this by hiding under my bed.'

She could hear the knocking on the front door, the butler opening and the approach of the footman to announce a guest. 'Margot. Please. You do not understand.'

'That is about to change, I think. We will all understand much more, if we speak to each other honestly. Now give permission to admit our guardian, or I shall call out to him that I am being held against my will.'

What was she to do? Justine gripped the edge of her lace pillow, twisting the velvet in her hands. Even the best servants were prone to gossip. To create a scene would make it all so much worse. When the footman announced Mr Montague, she gave the smallest of nods. And now the villain was in the room with them, his eyebrows arched in surprise at the presence of Margot.

He flashed a look in the direction of the servant, not wanting to speak until they were alone.

How much protection could the poor footman offer to them, should they need him? The boy was barely thirteen and Montague outweighed him by several stone. With another, helpless nod of her head, Justine dismissed him and instructed that the door be closed.

The moment it was, Montague dropped into a chair opposite them. His insolent slouch was meant to remind her how complete his mastery was over them and the situation they were in. 'Well played, Justine. I see now why you have been ignoring my instructions to meet.'

'I suspect she had been too busy, what with my arrival yesterday,' Margot responded for her, fancying herself the diplomat between two warring states.

'Silence, child.' Montague did not even glance in her direction, making it clear that she was a point of contention rather than a part of the discussion.

'I was ignoring your instructions because I did not wish to meet with you. In fact, I do not wish to see you, ever again. If you continue to threaten me, or my sister—'

'Justine!' The sharp rebuke came from Margot, who must think she was being overly dramatic.

'—I will tell Lord Felkirk all I know and accept the consequences for it.' She spoke louder, to be sure she could be heard over the protests of her sister.

'That would be extremely unwise,' Montague said, staring at her as though expecting he could shatter her resistance with a single icy stare.

'It is the only choice I have,' she said. 'I am but a weak woman, unable to settle my disputes with violence, as some do. Nor can I survive any longer on a diet of lies and deceptions.' To speak thus was the boldest thing she had done in her life.

She was rewarded with a flash of cold fury in his eyes and a momentary pause that told her he had no easy answer to this. It had never occurred to him that some day she might rise up and fight.

'Honesty is the best way to deal, in life or in business,' Margot said softly from her side, as though hoping her agreement would in some way bind the other two together.

'Yes,' responded Montague, seizing upon the words. 'If we are all to tell the truth, it is time for your sister to be honest with you and tell you what she has been willing to do to secure her place beside me in the shop. There is much you do not know, I think.' He looked to Justine then, in challenge. 'Is honesty still so attractive to you, I wonder?'

'We do not need to involve her in a thing which is just between the two of us,' Justine said. Surely he would not reveal the sordid nature of their relationship. It would reflect just as poorly on him as it did on her.

'If it involves the shop, it involves me as well,' Margot interrupted. She looked at Montague pleadingly. 'You have always promised me in your letters that I would help you there. I should have done so, long before now.'

'I gave your sister the power over that decision and she has refused to allow it,' Montague answered without hesitation.

She could not call him a liar, for the statement was at least a partial truth. 'His offer is not as it appears,' Justine said.

'You will not allow me?' Margot looked more than disappointed. She was furious. To her, it must appear as if Justine had no care for her wishes at all. 'You tell me time and time again that you do not want the shop. You do not like Bath.'

'Yet, she was willing to trade her virtue to keep her place there,' Montague announced, then feigned sorrow at the sudden revelation. 'You were always better suited to work at my side. But your sister would hear none of it. She used her beauty as a weapon against me. I knew what we were doing was wrong, but I could not resist.'

'That is not true,' Margot said. She was very still now, waiting for her sister to explain that it was all some horrible lie.

'That is not the way it happened,' Justine said. And it was not. She'd had no choice in the matter. To pick between her freedom or Margot's had been no choice at all. 'He forced me…'

'As I forced you to come here?' Montague countered. He turned to her sister again. 'You know she is pretending to be married to Felkirk, pretending to love him, engaging in Lord knows what vice. And all because she wants the diamonds.'

'Justine?' Justine watched as her sister's expression changed from doubt to horror. She believed him. How could she not? There was more than enough truth in what Montague was saying and it matched very closely to what she had told her sister.

But he had omitted one important detail. 'Montague struck him. With a poker. If I had not brought him home to heal, he'd have died on the floor of your precious shop and we would both have been hanged for murder.'

It was plain that the facts made the story no better. Margot stuffed a fist into her mouth, as though she could not decide whether to scream or be sick, but desperately wished to avoid either. Her hand muffled the sob that matched the tears starting in her eyes. Then she was up and gone, probably to her room, where she'd have been all along had she followed Justine's first order.

The door shut and silence fell in the room again, as though Montague expected her to speak first. Justine reflected that the wait for words could be prolonged, since she had no idea what to say next. Even if she managed to get him to leave again, it would take some time to calm her sister and to explain things in such a way that did not make her seem like a conniving whore.

Perhaps that was what she was, after all. She had thought herself the victim. But Montague's version of the truth seemed equally plausible. In either case, it was possible that her bond with her sister was irretrievably broken. Margot would never again look with trust upon either Justine or their guardian. Who did that leave to support and encourage her?

'What have you to say for yourself?' Montague said at last, as though dealing with a recalcitrant child. 'You see all the trouble you have caused, trying to get around me and disobeying my wishes? Next, I suppose you will tell me that you've learned nothing of the stones and the whole trip has been for naught.'

'Not for naught at all,' she said with a sigh. She sounded as tired as she felt. 'I have not had to endure your touch for several months. In my opinion, that is almost as good as a holiday.'

'Then your holiday is at an end,' he said, rising from the chair and standing over her. 'You will be coming away with me, today, while Felkirk is away and cannot ask questions. Tell your sister to pack as well. We are all going back to Bath.' There was something in his voice that made her wonder if that was their destination at all. Perhaps he meant to take them only part way. There was likely a cliff or a crag somewhere between there and here, where three might walk out and only one would return. He would be safe and there would be no more troublesome women, threatening unfortunate revelations.

'No,' she said, feeling rather proud of herself. 'I do not mean to stir a step from here. When Will comes back, I will tell him all and he can decide what is to be done with me.' She looked up at Montague, trying to raise some real defiance to disguise the apathy she felt creeping over her, now that all was lost. 'Since you cannot carry me bodily from the house, you might as well go away.'

'I will take your sister, then,' he said.

'She will be nearly as difficult to move as I am,' Justine said, with a slight smile. 'I suspect she is having hysterics in her room after what she has just heard from the pair of us. Better that you should go alone. You can travel faster that way and be far from here before my husband and the duke return.'

'Your husband?' Montague laughed at her.

It had been a stupid mistake. She must learn not to believe her own lies. 'Lord William Felkirk,' she corrected. 'The man you attacked. Perhaps he will not even seek you out, if I am here to take the blame for the crime.'

Montague considered for a moment and shook his head. 'You think you shall persuade him to forgive you, with your sad eyes, your bowed head and your gentle manners.' He reached out then and plucked the cap from her head, running his fingers through the curls and then pulling sharply back on them so that she was forced to meet his gaze. 'You will bind him with lust and pity, until he is as trapped by you as I have been. Then you will send him to find me and I will be the one who hangs.'

'Then I suggest you run as far and as fast as you can,' she said in a calm voice. She could feel the skin of her scalp pulled tight in his grip and the muscles in her neck straining against the force of his hands.

It did not matter. After today, she had likely lost the love of her sister. She would lose Will as well and the respect of everyone else she had met here. There was little left that Montague could do that would hurt her.

'I am not going anywhere,' Montague said with a smile. 'Unless it is back to the woods to await the return of your precious Felkirk.' He released her, pushing her roughly back into the cushions of the chair, and withdrew a pistol from his coat pocket. When he was sure she had seen, he dropped it back to where it had been hidden. 'How hard would it be, do you think, to finish him with a single shot?'

'Harder than you think,' she said breathlessly. 'He is with his brother the duke. There will be coachmen, outriders, livery. You cannot have so many bullets as that in your little gun.'

'Perhaps I shall wait until he rides out alone,' Montague replied. 'He is still weak, is he not? And probably just as careless as he was the day he turned his back on me.'

'You would not dare,' she said, suddenly quite sure he would.

'I would not act, unless you gave me reason. If you were to stay here, to blather the story to him, for example. Or if you plan on raising the alarm against me.' He paused, reaching for her again and running his thumb down her cheek. 'I would have no reason for it if you came away with me. Things will be as they were between us. Then, if it pleases me, we will discuss your freedom and that of your sister.'

Her heart sank. He would win, just as he always did. She would go with him, if only to lure him away from Will and Margot. If she did not, he would wait and watch, and eventually he would strike.

He could feel her weakening. It made him smile. 'Very good. I knew you would come to see things as I do. You of all people should understand what might happen to a man alone on that path. There are places that are shadowed, even in daylight. At night, when the moon is new as it was when your father died...'

'How did you...?'

'He thought he was too clever for me, just as you did,' Montague said. 'He hid the diamonds and carried nothing but an empty pouch. In the end, he gained nothing and lost his life. I got the insurance money, of course. But I wanted the stones as well.' His voice trailed off, as he thought back to the incident, his face marked by a childlike disappointment.

'You.' She felt no surprise. It was as if she had known, all along, but it had been too awful to contemplate, so she had refused to think too closely about it.

'Me,' he said, with a proud smile. Then he gripped her by her shoulders, pulling her to her feet. 'There is no point in resisting. I have been the architect of your fate for most of your life and I do not mean to change that now. In a few moments you will get your shawl and come away with me. You will leave this place and have no more contact with sweet William and his family. If you do anything to warn him, seek help of any kind, or reveal secrets that have been hidden for years, then things will be far worse than the lesson I mean to teach you now.' He kissed her, if such an open-mouthed punishment could be called a kiss. She fought, but the contact was relentless, his tongue pushed deep into her mouth until she was near to gagging on it and had ceased her struggles. Only then did he release her, following it with a slap that sent her reeling on to the sofa.

It was happening again. And as usual, she could think of no way to stop it. To cry out would mean discovery and an end to the assault. But it would also require explanations and the story would eventually get back to Will and then to his brother. The servants would not conceal an attack on their mistress from the very people who might punish the perpetrator.

There would be questions, so many questions. Why would she welcome such a man into the house? Why had she not called out sooner? And the question she asked herself most often: Why had she not found a way to stop this, years ago?

As usual, she had no answer. And as usual, she closed her eyes and imagined she was somewhere else.

Chapter Seventeen

Will needed only a moment to decide the route and speed for his return trip to the manor. Keeping a sedate pace on the road beside the carriage would give him time to think. He did not need to do that. He had spent too much time in the last weeks trying to understand the circumstances of his new life. But when one was basing one's cogitation on a horribly flawed series of supposed facts, one had nothing but nonsense at the end of it.

What he needed now was action, not thought. He set off cross country at a full gallop, through pastures and fields, scattering sheep and taking fences as a series of easy jumps. He had nothing to fear, after all. Jupiter was not dead. He had not fallen from a horse. And the injury he'd suffered was no accident.

He would arrive home much sooner than expected and surprise Justine de Bryun. The thought made him smile, but it was with none of the foolish, misplaced joy he'd been feeling lately. This was the kind of cold, grim satisfaction that thief takers must feel when they had their man dead to rights and heading towards the gallows.

He would arrive home and he would shake the truth out of her. He would ignore the huge, sad eyes and wistful smile, toss the lace into the fire and follow it with the ridiculous, prim cap she was likely wearing. A whore did not belong in modest gowns, nor did she bother to cover her head like a housewife. That she would sit with ladies under a scroll of virginal lace was an affront to him and his entire family.

She was a liar, nothing more than that. Below stairs, above stairs, and all the places in between. An image arose in his mind of the sweet, seemingly innocent face that had looked up at him as he'd touched her in their shared bed. Then he imagined that same face, smiling in a much more knowing way at Montague as they plotted against him. The beautiful body that had twined with his had writhed under another man, as she moaned with pleasure.

She was a liar and he had been a fool. Now it was not just her and Montague, but her sister he had to contend with. Lord knew if the girl was in any way involved in this. But was it really his problem, if she was not? He supposed she might be as big a victim as he was. All the same, it did not entitle her to much more than a ticket back to the school she supposedly attended.

The house was in sight now and he bore down on it, gaining speed, rather than slowing. After so long abandoned in a stall, Jupiter relished the speed, just as he did. But now he was eager to return to his own pasture and to be curried and cosseted by familiar hands. He stopped, still dancing with excitement, at the front door.

Will dismounted, handing the reins to a footman who could only manage an awed, 'My, lord', at the sight of the familiar, black stallion. Then Will pushed past him, into the house, to find his wife.

Not his wife, he reminded himself. No more weakness, no more foolishness. She was a madman's plaything, nothing more than that. Soon she would be gone. She and her lover would be in the hands of the law and life would return to normal.

When he opened the door of the morning room, the scene before him left his mind as blank as it had been when he'd first awoken. Justine was sprawled upon the couch, eyes shut tight from fear or pain, or both. Her face was dead pale, except for a red mark on one cheek, where a man's hand had slapped life into her complexion. Montague stood over her, radiating menace.

For a moment, Will could not think of anything, other than how wrong it was that such a thing should happen. Men did not hit women and they certainly did not do it while under his roof. That such a beautiful creature as his wife should have to fear anything, ever, was all the more wrong. Had he not promised her, over and over, that she would be safe with him?

He was halfway across the room, his hand already

raised to strike before he even remembered how satisfying it would be to hit this particular man, who had stolen six months of his life and ruined the one good thing that had come of it: his sweet and innocent Justine.

'No!' The word seemed to come, not from his mouth, but the very depths of his soul. With one hand, he gripped Montague by the shoulder and spun him. With the other, he struck. It was a full-armed cuff to the side of the head that sent Montague crashing to the floor.

'Will.' Justine's eyes were open now and he watched their expression change quickly from shock to relief, then change again to sorrow. Then she whispered, 'He has a gun. It is in his coat pocket.'

In response, he gave her a curt nod and focused on the man at his feet.

'If you stand, I will knock you down again. If you move for a weapon, I will break your hand with my boot. And do not think that I will turn my back on you, even for an instant. There will be no more chances to strike me from behind.'

Montague seemed barely bothered by this revelation. 'You finally remember, do you?' His lack of fear was unnerving.

'I remember it all, down to the last detail. You were a fool to bring my horse back to Wales, you know. It was bound to be discovered.'

Montague shrugged at this. 'Of all the things that would be my undoing, I did not think that would be the one. Do you mean to call the magistrate? It is your brother, is it not? He will arrest me and my mistress, and you will be free of us. I am sure it will be a terrible scandal and very embarrassing to all concerned. People will wonder that Bellston would be so easily fooled as to take a whore into the bosom of the family.'

Though Montague was mocking him, calling down the law would be the sensible thing to do. But now that justice was at hand, it felt strangely unsatisfying. There was something missing. Will resisted the urge to look back at the woman on the couch. If she was carted away to be punished for her crimes, he might never understand why she had gone to such lengths to trick him.

Instead, he stared down at Montague. 'You will hang, of course. Stealing my horse would be reason enough. But your list of crimes is longer than that. Attempted murder, fraud…'

'It is Justine who is guilty of fraud,' Montague supplied, as though trying to be helpful. 'It was her idea to come here, to masquerade as your wife, and to try to steal the diamonds you claimed to have found. If I hang, then she must as well.'

'He killed my father.' Justine spoke at last, her voice barely a whisper. 'Let justice be done.' If he turned to her, he would likely see that same, resigned, annoyingly obedient woman who had sat at his bedside and later come to his bed. Now she meant to go uncomplaining to the gallows.

Surely an innocent woman would have spirit enough to defend herself. Did she not understand that it would take only a word of entreaty and he would face down the devil himself to protect her?

But Montague was another matter entirely. Will glared down at him in disgust. 'I would much prefer that we settle this like gentlemen, if that is even possible. I know you prefer to strike men from behind and threaten women. If you can find someone foolish enough to stand with you, I will meet you at dawn.'

Montague laughed at this, as though the very idea of a duel was beyond him. 'And if not?'

'Then you will go to the gallows, just as you wish. Do not think to run. You will not cross the borders of my brother's land unnoticed.'

'That is not much of a choice,' Montague responded.

'It is the only one I am prepared to offer. With one, you stand a small chance of success and I can have my vengeance. If not, I shall turn you both over to the law and not think of it again. Although I would most like to be responsible for your death, I can live without the chance.'

'Then of course we shall duel,' Montague replied. 'And since Justine tells me you are weakened since the accident, I will choose swords. They are a weapon of a man with finesse. Very hard to handle when one's hand still shakes.'

'They are also more difficult to handle than a

fireplace poker,' Will said, pleased to see Montague flinch as the shot hit home.

By the time he answered, he had regained his aplomb. 'Very well, then. Swords at dawn. Send word of the location to the inn. Now, if you will excuse us?'

Will gave a slight tip of the head.

Montague stood and gestured to Justine. 'There is no need of a spy in your house, now that you are aware of her. Come, Justine.'

'The girl stays.' Will did not want to look at her, afraid of what he might see. Even now, she might be stirring on the couch, ready to return to her master.

Montague dropped his hand and shrugged. 'If you wish to keep her, she is yours. Until tomorrow, of course. Then I shall kill you and she will return to me. She will have no choice. Send word to the inn where you wish to meet and I shall see you at sunrise.' And then he was gone.

With the departure of Montague, a terrible stillness fell over the room. As if there was anything Justine could say that would explain or justify what had happened. Instead, she said the first words that came to her mind. 'How long have you known?'

'Just today,' Will said, still looking at the closed door. 'The coachmen found Jupiter yesterday, while bringing your sister to you.'

'And your memory came back?'

'All of it,' he said, turning to her with a grim

smile. 'Including the memory of you doing nothing to stop him, as he struck me down.'

That must be how it appeared to him. He would never believe her true feelings for him, if he remembered her from that day in Bath. Her future was destroyed. But perhaps there was a way that some good would come from this whole sordid mess. 'Margot had no part in any of it. She did not even know of my…intimate association with Mr Montague.'

'Is that all you have to say to me?' he said, with an ironic lift of his eyebrow. He took a seat on the opposite side of the room from her, as though he would keep as much distance from her as was possible. When he looked at her it was with the same, cynical appraisal he had used on the day they had met, in the shop in Bath, so many months ago.

She stared back at him, although not nearly as boldly. 'I have many things to say,' she admitted. 'But I can think of none that is more important than the welfare of my sister. What good would an apology do? There is no way to say I am sorry for the deception I have perpetrated. Mr Montague's assault on your person was so sudden that I did not know how to prevent it. To stop him from striking the second blow to finish you, I suggested that it would be better to bring you home so that I might steal the diamonds you claimed to have found.'

'And if you had found them?' he asked. 'Would you have gone back to him?'

'I meant to steal from him as well,' she said. 'To

take them and escape with Margot, to a place where he could not find us.'

'And the rest of it?' he said. 'Our elopement? My tragic accident?' He was sneering now, as though the very idea of a past with her disgusted him.

'I could think of no other way to explain myself.'

'And so you lied.'

'I lied,' she admitted.

'I suppose the things that happened when we were alone together were lies as well.'

'Would you believe me if I said they weren't?'

'Probably not,' he admitted.

Had she been hoping for a different answer? If so, her time here had made her foolish and overly optimistic. Perhaps it had been her imagination that his voice had softened, just for a moment, as though he, too, wished there could be a different end to this.

'Then all I can say to you is that I am sorry,' she said, at last. 'For hurting you and for tricking myself into believing my own lies. I should have admitted all, the day you awakened. I knew, from that moment, that this day would come. The longer I waited, the easier it became to pretend that there was a chance for happiness here. And now you hate me. I do not blame you.'

He said nothing in response and, in her mind, she cursed herself for wishing that he would offer some sop, to tell her she was wrong about his feelings. 'Now that we are at an end, I have but two requests.'

'You are not in a position to bargain with me over anything,' he said, emotionless.

'I know that. I deserve nothing, just as I have told you from the first moment we met. But I know you to be a good man, a kind man, a man of honour. As I said before, my sister had nothing to do with any of this. What I have done, from the first, I did for her.' She bowed her head. 'Do what you will with me, but do not punish Margot. At the very least, do not let her fall to the same unfortunate depths I have.'

He stared at her, without answering. Then he said, 'Your second request?'

'Do not duel with Montague.'

Will gave an incredulous laugh. 'You wish me to spare his life?'

'I wish you to protect your own.'

He made another disgusted noise. 'You have no faith in my abilities to defend myself.'

'On the contrary, I have infinite faith in Mr Montague's ability to turn a situation to his advantage. He will find a way to cheat. And then he will kill you.' She rose from the chair and sank to her knees before him. 'I would not see that happen for all the world. Have him arrested and be done with this.'

'They would take you as well,' he said. 'Do not think that I can protect you from this, for I do not know if that is possible.'

'Then let them take me,' she said, taking his hand in hers. When she squeezed it, she felt an answering grip. But there was no sign in his face that it was anything other than a reflex. 'Since I've been with you, I've had a lifetime of happiness. But that is over now. I must be punished for what I have done to you and your family. Let me go.'

It seemed he might not want to, for the grip on her hand was even stronger than it had been. Still, when he spoke, there was no sign of it in his voice. 'No matter what you might wish, I cannot go back on my word to Montague. If I could offer a challenge, and then take him unawares tonight, I would be no better than he is.'

'If you mean to throw your life away, then what was the point of saving you?' she said, pulling her hand away to wipe away a tear. 'If I had not stopped him, he'd have killed you in Bath and I would truly have been a murderer. Now you will be dead and I will have to go on, knowing I am to blame.'

'I am sorry to have inconvenienced you,' he said. He stood up and stepped around her. 'I am going to my room. I need to think. I will write to my brother and try to explain any of this.' He gave a vague gesture, as though it might be possible to draw a sensible version of events out of the air in front of him. Then he added, 'And I suppose I must think of something to do with your sister. At the very least, I can arrange to send her back to where she came from.'

It was such a small thing, yet it was more than she could have hoped for. 'Thank you,' she said, softly. 'In return, what do you wish me to do?'

'I have no idea. Nor do I care.' He gave a half-bow, as though he had rendered her a service of some kind. 'I am locking the door between our rooms, if that is what you are hinting at. Knowing what I do, I will not sleep easy if it is open. For the rest?' He shrugged. 'You are your own woman, Miss de Bryun. You are free of Montague and I no longer want you. What you do now is totally up to you.'

Chapter Eighteen

Will stared out of his bedroom watching the sun set through the first of the autumn leaves. It had been a lovely day. That it might be his last was a disappointment. But it could not be helped.

The righteous anger that had sped his journey home had disappeared like fog in sunlight, at the sight of Justine sprawled helpless before the angry Montague. In that moment, all he could remember was that she was his and she was in danger. Perhaps, tomorrow, she would laugh over his bleeding body and ride away with his killer. Today, in this house, he could only see the pale, beautiful woman who had watched over him as he suffered and came to his bed as though it was the only place she found happiness.

He should have called the servants, then called Adam and trusted it all to the law. Instead, he had informed his brother, in a terse note that his services would be needed in the morning, as a second. Since he had got no outraged response, he assumed that Adam had not yet returned from the inn.

Perhaps it was for the best. If Montague was left unwatched, he might decide to cut his losses and run. It would leave only Justine and her sister to deal with. That had best be done at a distance, with lawyers and bank drafts. One look into her beautiful green eyes and he would lose what was left of the common sense he had been so proud of and believe that they had actually been in love.

He stared at the door connecting their rooms. Despite what he had threatened, he had not locked it against her. Now he was possessed with the thought that she stood on the other side, ready to test the handle. If it opened, he would welcome her to his bed, just as he had every day that they'd lived here. Knowing what he did, it would be bittersweet to have her in his arms. But better that than the empty flavourless existence of a life without her. If she would just open that door and allow him some tattered scrap of pride, he could forgive anything and they would be together again.

There was a sharp rap upon his door, but it came from the hall and not her room. There was a moment of silence, then another knock, as though the person in the hallway had no time to waste. It was far too bold for a servant, but who else would it be?

When he opened it, he was surprised to see the younger Miss de Bryun staring up at him. Though nearly as lovely as her sister, Margot's looks were spoiled by a certain stubborn set of the mouth that promised continual strife to the man who did not let her have her way.

Without a word, she pushed past him, and sat upon the end of his bed. 'I need to speak with you, Lord Felkirk,' she said, swinging her feet impatiently.

'Then it would be far better that we do it in a public room,' he replied, standing by the open door. Did no one in Justine's family have an understanding of basic manners? Or was this another seductive trap?

'You are not in a public room,' she reminded him. 'You have not come out of this one all day. When I asked after you, the servants told me you were not to be disturbed.'

'It is plain you did not listen to them,' he said, closing the door and leaning against it.

'I cannot get Justine to talk to me, either,' Margot said with a frown. 'She is locked in her bedroom, weeping and writing what I expect is a tragic confession of her imagined sins. And no one will explain to me what is going on.' She glared at Will as though it was all somehow his fault. 'I am tired of listening to people who do not really say anything.'

'Perhaps they do not speak to you because what is happening is none of your business,' he said with a pointed look.

Margot's lips pursed with a stubbornness that almost diminished her loveliness. 'How would you know if it was my business or not? You hardly know me at all. I have no family but Justine and Mr Montague. Since they are two out of three of the persons involved in this problem, that is a clear majority.'

'Montague?' he said in surprise. 'You claim him as kin?'

'He is our guardian,' she said, with a frustrated huff. 'Surely you realised that.'

Will had nothing to say to this that did not indicate supreme ignorance, so he remained silent.

Margot continued to glare at him. 'He was my father's partner. When Mother died, he all but inherited us, along with the store.'

If that was true, his dear Justine's past was even more sordid than he'd suspected. 'That is no concern of mine,' he said, doing his best to contain his emotions. 'I do not know what your sister has told you, but I am not really her husband.'

'Of course she told me,' Margot said, speaking clearly as though she thought him slow of wit. 'I am her sister. She is not an open book. Until recently, I did not understand the depth of her troubles. But it is obvious that the two of you are well suited and very much in love. I urged her to explain everything to you immediately, so that you might be properly married.'

His mouth opened to deny her claim. But the only thought in his mind was a desire to question her further on the subject. What had her sister told her? Did Justine actually have feelings for him, or was that just another part of the lie?

Margot ignored his silence. 'I thought I understood the situation in Bath. But after what Montague said this afternoon, it is plain that too many secrets have been kept from me. And now you mean to keep secrets as well.'

'You spoke to Montague?' he said, surprised.

'I was there when he arrived,' she replied. 'Since my dear sister has denied me the truth, I blundered through the conversation, thinking he was nothing worse than a foolish old man with an unreturned penchant for Justine.'

'And what persuaded you otherwise?'

'When he announced that she had seduced him in an effort to keep me from returning to take my place in the business.' The girl shuddered in disgust. 'As if his word would be enough to turn me against one who has been like a mother to me since my birth.'

'You do not trust Montague?' he said.

'I did not distrust him,' she said cautiously, 'until today, at least. All I knew was that I was packed off to school as soon as it was deemed proper to send me, and I have hardly been home since.' She frowned again. 'I had hoped that there would at least be useful lessons, like bookkeeping. But instead, they attempted to teach me needlework, which I have no skill for, and French, which I already knew. It was an enormous waste of my time.'

Will ignored the girl's almost masculine views of education and turned the conversation back to the subject that interested him. 'If you were not home, you cannot possibly know what was going on between the two of them.'

At this she sighed. 'I know because, despite how everyone has been treating me, I am not some naïve child.'

'You are very young,' he argued.

Now she was looking at him as though he was the innocent in the room. 'You are fortunate, Lord Felkirk, that you were not born female. It is even worse to be born a pretty one, if you have no family to keep you safe. Our father died before I was born. And Mother was…' She paused again. 'She was not right. I remember a pale woman who did not speak and who died when I was almost ten, because she could find no reason to live. But through it all, I remember Justine, putting her needs aside and caring for me as a mother should care for a daughter. She warned me that men who talk loudest of chivalry will throw it aside in a heartbeat, if they see an opportunity to satisfy their desires without repercussion.'

'You have a very dark view of mankind, Miss de Bryun,' he answered.

'That is the fault of mankind, Lord Felkirk, for proving my sister right. I have known of Mr Montague's unwholesome interest in my sister for quite some time. But I had no idea that he would be so villainous as to act on it. If she wanted me to stay at school, she was likely ashamed…' For a moment, the girl's rather brusque manner faltered and she seemed on the edge of tears. Then she swallowed and went on. 'I had no idea that her warnings spoke from experience. If she refused to let me return home, it was because she feared for my safety there. And if she remained with Montague...'

The girl did cry now, pulling an already-damp handkerchief from her sleeve and wiping at her eyes. 'She would never have given herself to him willingly. And she would not have stayed with him had she not feared something even worse would happen should she leave. She should have let me come home. I'd have helped her.'

Will sat beside her and gave her a gentle pat on the arm, pressing his own dry handkerchief into her hand. Even in tears, she was pretty. In a few years, she would be as beautiful as her sister. But until she was of age, she had no choice but to accede to the wishes of her guardian, just as Justine had done. 'You needn't think that. After all, what could you have done?'

'I'd have killed him,' she said, vehemently. 'I'd have struck him down with the same poker he used on you, before I let him touch me. And I would not have let him hurt Justine, ever again. But she would not tell me the truth. She is not like me. She thinks of no one but herself, she never complains and she will not ask for help, no matter how much she needs it. She thinks she must be the strong one.'

He remembered her, in this very room, stroking his arm in the dark, kissing the scar as though the brand he bore was a mark of honour. It had been after the strange dream where she had demanded to be left alone. She had all but admitted the truth to him, talking of her difficult life.

At the time, he had been full of sympathy for her. He had vowed that he would keep her safe. But today, when she needed him, he had walked away as though she did not matter to him. Even after she had announced that she was willing to go to the gallows if it might spare him the risk of a duel, he had refused to trust her.

He took Margot by the hand and pulled her up from the mattress, walking her towards the door. 'Do not fear, little one. That time is over. From now on, I will be her strength.'

'Fine words,' she said, almost spitting them back at him. 'I have heard similarly vague promises from Mr Montague himself. But know, Lord Felkirk, that I will not allow you to treat my sister as he has done. She is not some pretty bauble to be used and discarded when you are bored with her.'

'That was never my intention,' he said softly.

'Intentions mean nothing,' she said, with a dismissive wave, 'if they are undone by one's actions. You claimed to love her. And yet, at the first sign of real trouble, you mean to cast her out.' She turned to glare at him. 'You will forgive me if I think my sister has suffered enough at the hands of men. In short, my lord, if you do not want her, do not think you can send her back to Montague with a clear conscience. It would be better to have her arrested and let her take her chances with the courts than to return her to the suffering she has endured from that monster.' And with that, she was gone, slamming the door so hard that even the stone walls seemed to shake.

Chapter Nineteen

'Justine.'

She woke with a start to find Will standing over her bed, a dim outline in the darkness. For a moment, she hoped that he had changed his mind and would gather her in his arms to assure her that it had all been a horrible dream. When he did not speak, the hope changed to fear. As she did with Montague, she lay perfectly still, feigning sleep and hoping that he would pass her by, just once.

'There is no point in pretending any more. I know you are awake,' he said, taking a taper from the bedside and lighting it with the last coals of the fire. 'Dress and come with me. There is something I must show you, before tomorrow.' Then he removed himself from her room, as though allowing the privacy to prepare herself.

Come back, she wanted to whisper. *Come back to me*. There was no need to be so distant. What had they not shared with each other, these last weeks?

Could they not have one last hour together? Even if he did nothing but sit silently in a chair while she dressed, it would be better than being alone.

But their time to be together had passed and the distance between them was more than just the space between their rooms. She had cried herself to sleep worrying about what was likely to happen when morning came. But not before writing a full account of what had happened in Bath, so she might give it to the duke. If Will brought a second, there would be no other man he might choose. Perhaps, if she delivered a full confession before the fight began, Bellston might call a halt to it and save Will's life.

She pulled on a gown and found stockings and shoes, wishing she had asked what it was that was expected. When she had seen him just now, he'd been fully dressed. But since it was the same coat he had worn in the afternoon, she suspected he had not gone to bed.

He should be resting. If he meant to carry out his foolish plan, dawn would come soon enough and he must be ready for it. Perhaps the duel was worrying him more than he let on. Perhaps he meant to run away with her. That was too much to hope for. There was something funereal in his demeanour that was far more frightening than his anger had been.

When she was finished dressing, she found him waiting in the hall for her, a candle in his hand to light their way. He preceded her down the steps and through the servant-less corridors to the main floor. The house was still asleep. The hall clock chimed three as they passed it, on their way to the back of the house.

From there, they went to the servants' stairs, down again, through the kitchens and beyond, down another flight of steps to a part of the house she had never seen. She could feel the cool air rising from the brick walls and see the racks upon racks of bottles. The wine cellar? 'Where are we going?' she finally raised the nerve to ask.

'To get you what you wanted, from the first moment you arrived here.'

For a moment, she could not think what that might be. Then she remembered.

The diamonds.

He had told the truth, in Bath, when he had claimed to know where they were. Their location had come back to him, with the rest of his memories. Then it would have been better had they stayed lost. 'It does not matter,' she said.

'Does it not?' He stared back at her. 'The stones I very nearly lost my life for have no value to you. I should think, given the things you were willing to do for them...'

'Stop!' If this was the last time she would be alone with him, she did not want to be reminded of what had happed. 'You know it has been more than that, for some time,' she said. There was no bitterness in her comment. It was too late for that.

If he knew, he did not want to admit it. There was a ghost of his old smile on his face, as though it had all been a huge joke. But the joke was over now, the memory fading. 'Well, in any case, if I have guessed rightly in their location, you shall have them.' His expression changed, yet again, to something different, solemn but peaceful. 'Should something happen this morning...to me, I mean...I want to make sure that you have what you have wanted from the first: your freedom. If there is trouble, you are to take them and your sister, and go.'

He turned back to focus on the way they were taking, turning left, then right between the racks to go deeper into the room. Justine followed in silence, her mind racing. At one time, what he'd offered would have been more than enough to satisfy her. She would not be punished for what had happened in Bath. She would not have to return to Montague. Her sister would be safe.

But the preface that had come before it was unbearable. He meant for her to have the jewels if he died. She could have said the same of her father, she supposed. It was likely his wife and daughters he had thought of, as he hid them from Montague. She was to have them at last. But if they cost her lover his life, it was far too high a price to pay for them.

They had come to a corner, to a heavy wooden door with an iron ring for a handle. He turned back to her, explaining. 'This part of the house is very old, hundreds of years, in fact. At that time, the place was more of a fortress than a home.' He pulled on the ring and the door, which looked so solid, swung easily open, revealing an arched stone hallway, stretching forward further than the light from the candle could reach. But from what she could see of it, it was swept clean and free of cobwebs. The gentle breeze coming from it was cold and fresh.

'This is the one thing that my mother wished she could have taken with her, when they built Bellston Court,' Will said, with a proud smile. 'After all this time, it is still dead useful. But not practical to replicate.' He led the way down the corridor and they walked for some minutes, until she was sure that they must have passed beyond the walls of the house. Not a corridor, then. It was a tunnel under the yard and it led in the direction of the woods.

'Adam and I played here, as children.' Will smiled at the memory. 'We were looking for Arthur, under his mountain. We were sure he must be here.'

'The raven,' she said, remembering the story he had told in the woods.

He nodded. 'It was a fever dream. But I was so very hot. I heard the maids crying over how I must surely die. I did not want to. I wanted to be cool again and I wanted Merlin's magic, so that I might live.'

'It is cool here,' she admitted, 'Even in the heat of the day, I'm sure.'

'And magical,' he insisted. They had come to the end of the tunnel, to another wooden door as large and heavy as the first one. He pushed it open and she saw starlight through tree branches, smelled the mossy scent of pine and loam and heard the low slap of water on rock.

'Be careful,' he said. 'Go left and there is a steep path, down to the pond. But right and up the hill…'

'The path through the trees,' she said.

'I opened the door and looked up. And I saw a man, tall and gaunt, with a black coat.'

'Your raven,' she said.

'Montague,' he answered. 'I must have surprised him, for he dropped this.' He reached into his pocket and pressed a scrap of velvet and silk into her hand.

She did not need light to know it for what it was. She'd handled hundreds of them, over the course of her time in the shop, bagging up loose stones in the little sacks, pulling the gold drawstrings tight so that all stayed clean and safe. She ran her fingers over the stitching, not needing the candlelight to see the ornate M and B intertwined and the tiny gold crown embroidered above it.

'I did not understand what it meant. I did not even find it in my pocket for another year. When I did, I told no one, because it was too late to do anything. They burned most of my playthings at the end of the summer, fearing that they were contaminated by my illness. I did not want to tell anyone of this for fear it would be taken from me and thrown into the fire. So I hid it in the nursery. And then I forgot.'

'I did not look in the nursery,' she said, surprised by her careless assumptions.

'Why would you? I had not been there in years

and I live in the house. But I was searching for a christening gift for Bill. And there it was.'

'And Montague dropped it,' she said, imagining the scene.

'He threw it, more like. As if he was angry. And then he saw me and was gone.' Will gave a low laugh. 'He must have thought he'd escaped unnoticed. Then, twenty years later, the little boy from Wales appears in his shop, holding the very same bag. No wonder he split my skull. He must have been very near to panic.'

'If he was angry because the bag was empty...' Justine said, trying not to be excited by the story.

'Then what happened to the diamonds?' Will was smiling broadly now, pleased that she was following his reasoning. 'If your father stumbled off the path and came upon this door, he might have gone inside.' Then he turned back into the tunnel, shining his candle along the wall to reveal another door, this one of metal. 'And he'd have found this.'

When he opened it, a blast of cold air struck her, causing her to pull the shawl tighter around her shoulders. 'The ice house?'

Will held his candle high, until he spotted a lantern set into a niche in the wall. He lit it, setting his candle beside it, to make as much light as he could. 'What better place to hide diamonds? It is so dark here that a robber would not find them unless he was led to the spot.'

'He hid them in the ice,' she said, wondering how they were to find them if that was true. The room was still a quarter full of huge blocks, layered with sawdust and hay. The flickering lantern light on the smooth wet surfaces cast weird blue shadows around the room. They seemed to dance in time to the soft, musical drip and trickle of melting ice.

'Most likely he tucked them into a crack in the wall, or dropped them on the floor. If he had put them in the ice, I suspect we'd have found a loose stone in the bottom of the ice-cream bucket by now.' He pulled a penknife from his pocket and searched through the ice-working tools on the hooks and shelves by the door to find something for her. He pressed an ice pick into her cold fingers. 'I could not look in spring, when I first had the idea. Winter had just passed and the room was full to the doorway. But it is very near to the time of year when your father died. The same spaces are exposed.' Then he turned her gently to face into the room. 'Now, you must imagine that you are your own father. You have only a few moments to conceal something of value. Where would you put it?'

He lifted the lantern high over his head, so she could see the details of the room. While the tunnel leading to it was mortared stone, this space had been carved directly into the rock under the hillock. The walls were marked with the fissures and cracks of the excavation, any one of which could hide the jewels. Under her feet, the layer of damp sawdust that had frozen to the ground was thick enough to con-

ceal any manner of things. If they had not been discovered for all this time, then what chance had she?

Then she remembered Will's words. She must
think like her father. She had no trouble picturing
him walking the path above. She had done it before. But now she imagined it not bright with morning sunshine, but gathering gloom. She was being
stalked. She could feel the eyes on the back of her
neck. But the silence of the approach told her the
identity of the assailant. Montague meant to be-
tray her. She felt her quickening pulse and the over-
whelming desire to run.

If she did, he would catch her easily and take what
he wanted, just as he always did. She must not give
way to panic. Her father had kept a cool head, even
when death was imminent. He might have lost his
life, but he had denied Montague what he'd most
wanted. The thought made her smile. It gave her
strength.

She looked around the room again. 'It would have
been dark. There was no time to light a candle. And
he did not want to be discovered.' She closed her
eyes tight, to shut out the lantern light, and reached
out a hand. Ice in front of her. It was shockingly
cold and she drew back quickly, until her shoulders
were against the wall behind her. Her hand bumped
against a shelf.

That would be far too obvious.

She worked her way along the wall, trailing hands
against it, following it around the corner until she

had worked herself into what little space there was between the stacked ice blocks and the wall. Then she felt for a likely hiding place. There was nothing here. She could not find a notch to hide a single stone, much less a handful.

And then she remembered her father. When she had last seen him, he'd seemed huge to her, like a great blond bear. She had been but five. But it had been more than imagination. He had been a large man who could not have wedged himself so deeply into this space. She moved back towards the door again, until there was barely enough space for a large man. Then she ran her hands over the bumps and crevices in the wall. That was when she found the crack. It was large at the top and even larger near the floor. But in the middle, at a place about equal with the height of her shoulders, it narrowed. While much of the wall was rimed with frost, the ice in this particular place was hard and smooth. She opened her eyes, but it was too dark to see much more than what she had discovered with her touch. 'Here,' she said, tapping the ice with the pick in her hand. 'Bring the lantern.'

Will crowded close behind her, holding the light so it shone over her shoulder.

Without thinking, she leaned back into him, trying to steal some warmth from his body to fight the growing chill of being so close to the ice.

Had he forgotten that he hated her? It almost seemed so. He did not draw away from her, but pulled her closer to shield her from the cold as she worked.

Her hand trembled as she jabbed the pick into the ice, only to feel it slide away without leaving so much as a chip. She struck harder the next time. And harder still after that. The ice in this spot was solid, as if it had rested there until it was as hard as the rock around it. Compared to all the other problems that had come between her and her goals, it was a very small thing. But it was very annoying. She struck harder, again and again.

And then she gasped. Just for a moment, she thought she had seen a glittering that was brighter than frozen water. She took her lover's hand and directed it, to form a cup at the base of the crack. She struck one last time, prying outwards to lever out the last of the ice. And what looked, at first glance, like a trickle of water, split into a multitude of tiny sparkles.

She heard Will's laugh of satisfaction as the gems poured into his hand. She poked about for a moment longer to be sure that nothing remained hidden between the rocks. Then she ran a fingertip through the shavings of frost and felt the sharp edges of faceted stones. If she got her jeweller's loupe and looked closer, she was sure she would recognise her father's work in the cuts, just as she could when she looked at the stock from Montague's safe.

She glanced down at the little velvet pouch, still dangling from her left wrist like a reticule, and opened it so that Will might tip his hand and pour the stones inside. Then she tightened the drawstring and offered him the bag.

He shook his head. 'Now that you have them, they are back where they belong.'

'Not quite,' said a voice behind them.

Chapter Twenty

'Montague.' Will let out a curse under his breath at the sight of the man and the pistol he held pointed at them. 'How did you find us?'

Justine berated herself for being so foolish as to lower her guard, even as she'd imagined his silent approach. She had warned Will that the man would find a way to cheat. But what was the point of winning the duel if he left Wales without the diamonds? 'He waited in the woods and saw us when you opened the tunnel door.'

Montague gave a slight bow of acknowledgement, as though proud of his cleverness. 'When you said you remembered all, I knew you would get the stones before it was too late. I had but to wait where the murder occurred to see if you would come and lead me to them.'

'I should have remembered to lock the door behind me,' Will said with a scowl. 'You have already proven that you are a coward who will creep along behind, waiting for a chance to take from the un-wary.'

Montague shrugged. 'Not as noble as your family would be. But my method has proven effective so far. Now give me the diamonds and we will be almost finished here.'

'Almost?' Will said, watching the pistol in his hand.

'There is still the matter of your threats of prosecution and the impending duel.' Montague smiled. 'While the odds are in my favour, I would not like to leave killing you to chance.'

She and Will had turned as a couple and she still stood slightly in front of him. Now he was taking her by the shoulders, trying to move her behind him, out of the line of fire.

That would not do. If she moved, her guardian would have a clear shot. She planted her feet and refused to budge. 'Have you forgotten that you have but one bullet in your little gun?' she said.

'I need but one,' Montague said. 'Once William Felkirk is dead, the duke will want justice. And no tale of lost diamonds and evil strangers will save you from the hangman's noose. It does not matter to me if you stay or come away with me, Justine. But leaving Wales might be the more sensible choice.'

Will gripped her firmly by the shoulders again, still trying to move her behind him. 'Perhaps we could continue this conversation in a place where the lady is not trapped between us.'

'The lady?' At this, Montague laughed. 'You poor deluded fool, that you should still call her that now that you remember what she was to me. Justine will move of her own accord, soon enough. Once she has worked out, with her tiny, feminine brain, how hopeless her situation is, she will come back to me and leave you to die. Like all women of her type, she cares for no one but herself.'

After killing her father, forcing her into a life she did not want, and threatening the only two people she loved, was that really what he thought of her? The idea that she would come tamely to his side and resume her old life was a sign of madness. Or perhaps it was only stupidity. Margot was safe, no matter what had happened. Will had promised her that, even when he was so angry he could hardly look at her. But without Will, she would have nothing left to lose. When one did not care about the future, there were far better alternatives than sharing a bed with a man she despised.

Justine watched as Montague's gun hand twitched ever so slightly, as though trying to decide if it were possible to shoot past her and hit his target. She was too small to be an adequate shield for him, especially when Will seemed intent on being the protector, not the protected. He was still tugging at her arm, trying to ease her out of the line of fire.

She spread her arms wide, trying to cover as much of him as she could, staring at the hand that held the gun, watching for the telltale tightening of tendon and muscle. Her own hands clenched in response. The slight movement set the bag that held the diamonds swinging slowly on her wrist. It was too light to be a weapon. But perhaps…

She extended her arm suddenly and twisted her wrist. The drawstring slipped down her hand and the bag fly off her arm, arching through the air to land behind Montague. 'Here are your diamonds. Take them and go.'

He was not distracted, as he should have been. Instead, the movement had startled him. He raised the gun, finger on the trigger.

He was going to shoot and it was her fault. Without thinking, she threw herself forward, as though it might be possible to stop what was surely to occur. Then she remembered the ice pick, still clutched in her right hand, and fell forward, holding it in front of her.

There was a noise, very close and very loud. Then Montague's body weighed heavy against hers, as they fell to the wet ground. The warm, wet ground. That could not be right. An ice house should not be warm. Will was standing over her, the lantern swinging wildly in his hand, casting shadows against walls and ceiling, and over his very white face. He was so very pale. But at least he was still alive. He was moving his lips, but she could not seem to hear what he was saying. It was easier, just to close her eyes and think of something else.

Chapter Twenty-One

'Justine! Oh, my God. Justine!' He had been hatching a plan to get clear of her and wrestle the gun from Montague. He had not been paying attention to her. That had been Montague's problem as well, he was sure. Neither of them had given her enough credit. Nor had they expected her to spring like a tiger for the throat of the man who had persecuted her.

God help him, there had been a shot. His head was still ringing with it. The foolish girl had given no thought to her own safety, throwing herself at an armed man. She might have been injured, even killed. If she had been lost because of his slow reflexes...

He was at her side in an instant, rolling Montague's inert body to the side so that he might tend to her. 'My darling, are you all right?' Was she his darling? He hadn't thought so, this afternoon. But why else would she risk her life to protect him? 'Justine?'

She stared blankly up at him without answering.

Had she been shot? There was a prodigious quantity of blood, but it did not seem to be hers. He ran his hands carefully over her body, looking for tears in her garments, or the flinch and cry as his fingers accidentally probed a wound. But she could not seem to feel them at all. Her flesh was impassive at his touch, cold, but whole.

'Justine.' Then he remembered the shot, so near to her ear. 'I think you have been deafened by the gunshot, love. Do not fear. It will be better soon.'

Perhaps she had heard that, for she closed her eyes, as if to shut out the scene.

It was just as well. If she was not already aware of it, he did not want her seeing what she had done. Now that Will had moved him, Montague lay on his back, eyes wide and sightless, the blood pooling behind him, the ice pick buried to the handle in his chest.

He must warn the servants, before some maid wandered down to fill an ice bucket and frightened herself witless. And a man must come to take care of the corpse in the ice house. Although, until he could be buried, this was the best place for him.

And, of course, someone must be sent to the big house to get the duke so that he might swear a statement, or whatever one did when a crime occurred. There would be no question of self-defence, for the gun Montague had threatened them with was still clutched in one lifeless hand.

The little bag that held the loose stones lay just at the edge of the spreading pool of blood. Will scooped it up and dropped it in his pocket. Then he gathered up the real treasure: the body of his precious Justine. She was limp in his arms and so very cold. Was that the fault of the ice around them, or was it shock?

It was no trouble getting her back down the tunnel, through the kitchen and back up the stairs to her room. Once there, he did not bother with the maid, but stripped the bloody gown over her head and threw it into the fireplace, shifting the coals and poking it until he was sure it would catch and burn.

From behind him, he heard her soft voice. 'You oughtn't to have done that. It is probably evidence of some kind.'

He turned to see her staring into the fire. Her expression was still frighteningly blank, as though she could not quite understand what she was seeing. But he was relieved to see some colour returning to her face. 'My word to my brother will be evidence enough, I am sure. You will not be forced to sit like Lady Macbeth, covered in gore.'

'I do not think the blood on her hands was real,' she said, staring down in puzzlement at her own hands, which were quite literally stained.

Will filled the basin and brought it to her along with a towel, that she might wash. When she made no move to do it, he helped her, wiping away every last trace of what had happened. He took the basin away again, dumping it in the yard so there would be no trace of the pink-tinged water. Then he brought a dressing gown, wrapping her tight so that she would not take a chill, and a glass of brandy from a decanter he kept in his room. He added a few drops of the laudanum the doctor had left for his headaches and swirled the liquor in the glass. While he normally did not believe in the need for soporifics, his head wound was nothing compared to what she must have suffered in the last day. He pushed the glass into her limp hand, wrapping the fingers around the stem, and said, 'Drink.'

She refused at first. But he would not release her until she took it and coughed it down. 'You do not have to wait upon me, hand and foot,' she said, rising as if to prove it and sinking weakly back on to the bed.

'And you did not have to save my life,' he said. 'All the same, I am glad you did.' He lifted her legs to swing them up on to the bed and covered her, fluffing the pillows behind her head. 'Rest.'

'But I must speak to someone, to explain… And I need to tell you…' Her brow creased as though she could not think what it was that she meant to say.

'You will do that in the morning,' he assured her. 'For now, I will call Margot to sit with you, in case you need company in the night.' He kissed her lightly on the cheek. 'And then you will go to sleep, Justine. No arguments.'

'Yes, Will,' she said softly and closed her eyes.

Justine woke the next morning, her mind woolly, her thoughts confused. Most notably, she was surprised to be waking, for it meant that she had man-

aged to fall asleep. As Will had carried her into the
room, she had half-feared that she would never be
able to close her eyes again, much less free her mind
long enough to get any rest.

Perhaps he had put something in the brandy he
had given her. Or perhaps it was the sight and sound
of her sister, sitting beside the bed and struggling
with the thread and bobbins in the dim candlelight,
as though attempting to prove that she had any interest in the skills Justine had been trying to teach her.

'You needn't bother,' Justine had told her, gently.

'I know that,' Margot had answered, frowning
down at the lace in a way that would have seemed
very bad tempered of her, had Justine not seen the
expression on her face almost since birth.

'The things Mr Montague said about my trying
to keep you from your place in the shop...'

Margot had looked up at her with the same direct,
no-nonsense expression she often wore. 'Mr Montague was a villain. He is gone now and we needn't
worry ourselves about what he did or did not say.
In fact, I recommend we do not think of him at all.'
Then she smiled more softly. 'It is just the two of
us, Justine, as it has always been. The two of us and
your Lord Felkirk, of course.'

'Of course,' Justine said, dutifully, thinking that
it remained to be seen whether she had a Lord Felkirk or not. Will had been very gentle with her, as he
had put her to bed. He could just as easily have left
her in the ice house and called for the duke. Perhaps

he was merely grateful for the action she had taken to defend him.

As he'd carried her, she had felt the tear in the shoulder of his jacket that the bullet had made as it had flown past his head. Only a few inches down, or to the left, and it would have struck him. It did not matter what happened to her now, as long as she knew he was safe and Montague could not hurt him again.

It would be nice if he had forgiven her, even in a small way, for concealing the truth from him. But there was a limit to how much a man could forget, especially one who had been trying for weeks to remember the past.

She had done an awful thing to Mr Montague. But perhaps it was mitigated since she had prevented him from doing something even worse. And though murder was by far the most serious of crimes, she had done many horrible things already. No matter how hard she had tried, she simply was not a very good person. She was a murderer, a schemer and a fallen woman. All the good behaviour from this moment on would not erase any of it.

It shocked her even more to know that she did not regret what had happened with her guardian in the ice house. If she had been the sort of proper woman that Will deserved, she would have been distraught over what she had done. It had been awful. But every moment she'd spent with Montague had been nearly as terrible. There was a strange peace in knowing that, having done the worst thing possible, she would not see him, ever again.

With no particular plan, she got up and woke Margot, who was dozing in a chair beside the bed, a trail of tangled silk threads trailing from the pillow in her lap, the lace pins scattered on the carpet at her feet. Justine kissed her lightly on the cheek and sent her back to her own room to get some rest. Then she called for the maid and dressed with care in her simplest of muslin gowns, a pale yellow patterned with tiny oak leaves. The maid finished by pinning her hair up beneath a plain linen cap.

Justine looked at herself in the cheval glass. She declared the look suitable for a morning walk to either the wood, or to prison. Was there a prison within walking distance, or would she be driven there? She imagined herself in the back of a cart, driven down the high street of the village, displayed before all as a criminal.

She smiled and turned away. With such a dramatic imagination, she should be writing novels of her own. This one sounded like the sort where the fallen woman died in jail, after writing lengthy apologies to God and man for crimes which were caused by the actions of others. Family and friends, and the handsome hero all mourned her loss, though none of them had done a thing to help her when she was alive and with them.

While she had no objection to confession, she would offer no more apologies. Had she been forced to live her life again, it would most likely have gone much the same. Many of the choices had been forced upon her. Others, like the decision to come to Wales and give herself to Will Felkirk... No matter how wrong it had gone in the end, she could not bring herself to regret it. She reached up and plucked the cap from her head, dropping it to the floor beside the bed. Then she left her room and went down to meet her fate, head unbowed and uncovered.

She found Will and the duke in the study, a light breakfast on the desk between them. The diamond pouch lay there as well, leaning casually against the sugar box as though loose diamonds were but one more thing that the aristocracy sprinkled into their tea.

At her entrance, both men rose and Will said, 'Will you join us, Miss de Bryun? And close the door behind you,' he added, glancing towards the hall to make sure no one had heard.

Miss de Bryun. That was her name. But she could not think when she had heard it pronounced in that particular tone. Perhaps this was what she'd have heard in that imaginary meeting between herself and a pleasant young man in a shop in Bath.

'My lord,' she said, closed the door and curtsied. 'Your Grace.' She had done that wrong. She should probably have acknowledged the duke before his brother. But there had been no duke in her fairy-tale meetings. Nor had she needed to plead before one for life and liberty.

Will got a chair and pulled it up to a corner of the desk, then seated her and passed a third plate and the toast rack. There was a third teacup as well. They had expected her and had not wanted to disturb the conversation with the comings and goings of servants.

'My brother has given his version of the morning's events,' the duke said, sipping his tea with no sign of anxiety. 'Since I trust him, we will spare you the repeating of what must have been a most traumatic event. For the purpose of the inquest, I will say that an intruder threatened you both and met with an unfortunate end. Since he was also responsible for a murder on the property some years ago, and an earlier attack on my brother, we have been saved the price of the rope needed to hang him.' He gave her a pointed look. 'And that is all that will be said about that.'

'Thank you, your Grace.' Was it really to be so easy as that? She deserved some sort of punishment for taking Mr Montague from the world, even though it was a great relief to think that she would never see him, or hear his voice again.

'Did the man have family?' Bellston asked. 'Was there any that we need notify?'

'None but my sister and myself. He was our guardian, when our mother died, and in charge of our affairs.'

'Your guardian,' the duke repeated, clearly appalled.

'He was not just my father's partner, but his oldest

and dearest friend. In Father's will, he was charged with the keeping of the business and of our family. And when my mother died…' She swallowed. 'We went to him, hoping he would be like a father to us. That was not the case.'

Beside her, Will cursed beneath his breath.

'When you came of age,' the duke said, regaining his composure, 'why did you not leave?'

Will gave a warning growl in the direction of his brother. Clearly, he did not like the line of questioning. The duke held up a hand. 'Silence, William. I have other questions about recent events involving Miss de Bryun. I mean to have them answered to my satisfaction.'

Justine gave them both an encouraging nod. It had all been very polite and rational so far and not the barrage of shouted accusations she had imagined. 'When I came of age, there was still my sister to consider. Until she came of age as well…' She busied herself with the marmalade pot, trying not to think of all the horrible things that might have occurred '…I could not leave her alone in his care.'

'And when you came to my home under false pretences and lied to Penelope and I, pretending to be my brother's wife?'

'Lord Felkirk was bleeding and near death. But he had not yet expired and I did not wish to be an accessory to his murder. If he could be healed, I would attempt it. But if he was to die, it would be better that he did it in the presence of his family.

Lying about our relationship was a bad idea, but on the journey here I could not manage to think of a better one.'

The duke sat quite still for a moment, thinking. 'Nor can I,' he said. 'Considering all the evidence, I have no real desire to prosecute you. Saving my brother's life on at least two occasions tips the balance in your favour. As to some of the more unsavoury parts of this story, I will leave them to you to explain or conceal from my wife and friends, as you see fit.'

'Thank you, your Grace,' she said, rising as he rose and curtsying again.

Now that business was done, Bellston seemed to relax again into the more brotherly figure she had grown accustomed to seeing. 'I will leave you and Miss de Bryun alone now, Will. I am sure you have much to talk about.'

'We do, indeed,' Will said and rose to walk him to the door.

Once they were both gone from the room, Justine relaxed back into her chair, surprised to find her hands trembling as they raised her teacup. She had avoided prosecution. At one time, it was all she had hoped for. But who knew there would be so much to lose?

Will returned to the room and took his chair beside her again, putting his hands on his knees and sighing in satisfaction. 'That went well, I think,'

'Better than I'd hoped,' she said, setting down the

cup, careful that it did not rattle against the saucer as she did so.

'Now that Montague is gone, you and your sister are free to do as you like.'

Free. Justine rather liked the sound of the word. But it bothered her that he could be so cavalier about her freedom. Had her dependence on him been such a burden?

'My brother has agreed to help with any legal matters concerning the transfer of the shop to your full ownership. He will take the guardianship of your sister upon himself, until she is of age. The diamonds are yours, as well,' he added, sliding the pouch across the desk to her.

'Mine.' This was what she had wanted from the first. Why, now that she had achieved her goal, did it seem valueless?

'Well, in truth, they likely belong to the insurance company. Montague would not have gone to the trouble of trying to take them if he had not meant to file a claim. But even after they are reimbursed, you may see a considerable profit from their increased value.' Will was talking quite sensibly of things that would have interested Margot far more than they did her. The details of the transfer were probably important. Perhaps focusing on them would relieve the feelings of panic at being alone with the man whom she had tricked.

'What am I to do with a jewellery shop?' she said, baffled. 'I know how to purchase and grade the stones, of course, but Montague was the designer and goldsmith. And there are the books to be kept, employees to pay, customers to please...' There was so very much work. And it was all a very long way from Wales.

'You could always sell it,' he suggested. 'Or hire a manager until your sister is ready to take control.'

'I suppose it is too much to hope that she will forget her plan and find a husband,' Justine said, staring into the bottom of her empty cup.

'She seems very set on the idea of keeping it. In any case, you may settle it between the two of you,' Will said softly. 'It is your decision, and yours alone. But I suspect, what with a successful business and a safe full of jewellery, that you are now a wealthy woman, Miss de Bryun.' He cleared his throat. 'You shall have your pick of young men, should you wish to marry.'

'Marry.' Did he really need to remind her of the fact that they were not attached? Each time he called her Miss de Bryun, it was as if he hammered nails into her heart. What good would it be to finally have control over one's own life, when one could still not have what one truly desired? 'I will not marry,' she said softly. After Will, she could not bear the thought.

'It would be a shame if you did not,' he said.

'Now that you know my past, you must understand that it would not be possible.'

'I am part of that past,' he reminded her.

He was. But if he was the past, then what point was there in finding a future?

He cleared his throat and shifted uneasily in his chair. 'No matter what you choose, I do not wish the events of the last few weeks to weigh too heavily on you. You are free, just as I said before.'

Was this what freedom was? To be alone and heavy hearted? If so, then she did not want it after all.

'If a child results, of course I will claim it.' He was talking quickly, as though wanting to get through all the difficult words that would separate them, before she could raise an objection. 'For my part, I would be willing to forget the whole affair. No word of it shall ever pass my lips.'

'You mean to forget me?' Perhaps it was all the talk of freedom going to her head. She had expected a dismissal. She had even been prepared for it. But now that it was here, she could not manage to go meekly. 'How convenient for you, William Felkirk, that you have such a porous memory. If you insist on forgetting anything, why could it not be everything that had happened before the last two weeks?'

'You misunderstand me,' he said hurriedly.

She ignored his interruptions. 'You were quite happy to lie with me when you could not remember how we had met. But now that you know of my past, which was no fault of mine, you would forget me, as though I was never here. I was a fool to allow myself to believe, even for a moment, that a wonderful man like you might love me, in spite of what had happened. I—'

Suddenly, he pulled her out of her chair and into his lap. Warm, strong lips on hers cut off any desire to argue. As it had been for some days, during their kisses, they were in total agreement with each other. One of his hands cupped her bottom and the other plucked at the pins that still held her hair, eager to touch it now that there was no cap in the way.

He pulled back and shook his head in wonder at how out of hand things could get with a single kiss. 'It was so much easier, when I thought you were my wife. Then I simply assumed that you would obey me and commanded that you come to bed. But now I have no right to hold you.' To her surprise, his face was suffused with a schoolboy's blush. 'When I look into your eyes, I can barely find the words...' He smiled. 'Now that I have your attention, may I be allowed to speak in my defence?'

She nodded cautiously, afraid that if she moved too much, he would come to his senses and return her to her own chair.

'As I have been trying to tell you, the decision is yours, just as it should have been from the first. You did not come willingly to my house or my bed. I will not force you to stay here, if you would prefer to be elsewhere. And I am hesitant to even offer this, for it is quite possible, when the accounts are totalled, that you will be worth more than I am. I would not want to be thought a fortune hunter. Nor would I press my advantage to force you into a union that might disgust you…'

She kissed him back to prove that she was most definitely not disgusted. In fact, his words were so sweet she was trembling in his arms. Or else she was finally giving in to the terror she had felt over the last twenty-four hours, when she was sure she would lose him.

In answer, his hands became less demanding and wrapped loosely around her, offering protection and support, as his kisses soothed her brow. 'It is all right,' he whispered. 'You are safe now. If you stay with me, I promise you need never worry again.'

'My past.'

'You have none. Nor do I.' He buried his face in her throat, pressing his lips to her skin. 'My life began when I opened my eyes and saw you leaning over my bed.'

'Suppose we met, just as I imagined,' she said dreamily. 'Quite innocently, in a shop in Bath?'

He smiled. 'I would have been struck mute by your beauty and would probably have embarrassed myself by talking nonsense as I did just now.'

'I'd have thought it charming,' she said.

'But you'd have been too proper to respond,' he replied. 'From what I have seen, you are a very reserved young lady, with your prim dresses and your silly caps.'

'I would not have been wearing a cap,' she reminded him. 'They are for married ladies. It is why I no longer wear one.'

He stroked her head. 'Then I am glad that you are unmarried, for I do love to touch your hair.'

'I would not wear one, if my husband wished otherwise,' she said. 'You must realise by now what an agreeable wife I would be.'

'Wife,' he said, purring the word into the skin of her neck. 'That is what I wish you to be. I had grand plans to court you slowly and properly, so you might come to me by your own choice. But it seems I am just as impulsive as you made me out to be, when you invented our elopement. Come away with me, Justine. We will go to Scotland this very day and marry over the anvil. We will bring our families this time to witness it. Other than that, it will be just as you imagined it.'

She would be married, just as she had dreamed. And it would be to the man she loved, more than life itself. 'Almost as I imagined it,' she reminded him. 'In my story, we were forced to marry because you could not contain your desire and seduced me.'

He smiled and she felt the hand on her hip tighten, ever so slightly. 'I had forgotten,' he said, pushing her from his lap so that he could stand. And then, before she could protest, he has scooped her up in his arms and was carrying her towards the door. 'Let us retire to my chamber, Miss de Bryun, and I will show you just how it happened.'

* * * * *

REQUEST YOUR
FREE BOOKS!

 HARLEQUIN® HISTORICAL:
Where love is timeless

2 FREE NOVELS PLUS 2 FREE GIFTS!

YES! Please send me 2 FREE Harlequin® Historical novels and my 2 FREE gifts (gifts are worth about $10). After receiving them, if I don't wish to receive any more books, I can return the shipping statement marked "cancel." If I don't cancel, I will receive 6 brand-new novels every month and be billed just $5.44 per book in the U.S. or $5.74 per book in Canada. That's a savings of at least 16% off the cover price! It's quite a bargain! Shipping and handling is just 50¢ per book in the U.S. and 75¢ per book in Canada.* I understand that accepting the 2 free books and gifts places me under no obligation to buy anything. I can always return a shipment and cancel at any time. Even if I never buy another book, the two free books and gifts are mine to keep forever.

246/349 HDN F4ZY

Name	(PLEASE PRINT)	

Address		Apt. #

City	State/Prov.	Zip/Postal Code

Signature (if under 18, a parent or guardian must sign)

Mail to the **Harlequin® Reader Service:**
IN U.S.A.: P.O. Box 1867, Buffalo, NY 14240-1867
IN CANADA: P.O. Box 609, Fort Erie, Ontario L2A 5X3

Want to try two free books from another line?
Call 1-800-873-8635 or visit www.ReaderService.com.

* Terms and prices subject to change without notice. Prices do not include applicable taxes. Sales tax applicable in N.Y. Canadian residents will be charged applicable taxes. Offer not valid in Quebec. This offer is limited to one order per household. Not valid for current subscribers to Harlequin Historical books. All orders subject to credit approval. Credit or debit balances in a customer's account(s) may be offset by any other outstanding balance owed by or to the customer. Please allow 4 to 6 weeks for delivery. Offer available while quantities last.

Your Privacy—The Harlequin® Reader Service is committed to protecting your privacy. Our Privacy Policy is available online at www.ReaderService.com or upon request from the Harlequin Reader Service.

We make a portion of our mailing list available to reputable third parties that offer products we believe may interest you. If you prefer that we not exchange your name with third parties, or if you wish to clarify or modify your communication preferences, please visit us at www.ReaderService.com/consumerschoice or write to us at Harlequin Reader Service Preference Service, P.O. Box 9062, Buffalo, NY 14269. Include your complete name and address.

HHI3R

They moved on to the parlor, piling the mantel with holly and ivy.

He glanced down at her. "You are smiling again, Mrs. Marsh. Twice in one day. It must truly be Christmas."

Was it really so rare a thing to see her smile? She hoped not. But now that he had commented on it, she could not manage to raise the corners of her lips to prove him wrong.

The duke sighed. "And now it is gone again. Do you think if we put up a kissing bough it will come back?"

"Certainly not." At least he had given her a reason to frown. All the kindness in the world did not give him the right to tease her.

"You have several fine arches, and a hook in the center of the parlor where you might hang it." He glanced up in mock sadness at the empty door frames. "And yet, I see none there."

"That is because there is no point in hanging something of that kind in this house," she said firmly, as though the matter was settled. "There is no one here that wants or needs kissing."

"Really," he said, surprised.

"My son is too young to care. If I allow my daughter to run riot I will have even more trouble than I do already. The servants have no right to be distracted with it for half the month of December."

"And you?" he prompted.

"I?" She did her best to pretend that the thought had not occurred to her. She turned away. "It is foolishness, and I have no time for that, either."

"Perhaps it is time to make the time," he said, stepping forward, holding the branch above her head and kissing her on the lips before she could object.

It was as if the world had been spinning at a mad rate and suddenly stopped, leaving her vision unnaturally clear. She was not a minor character waiting in the wings of her own life. She was standing in the center of the stage, alone except for the duke.

And then it was over. A strange, adolescent awkwardness fell over them. He cleared his throat. She straightened her skirt. They both glanced at the door and then back to each other. "I trust I have demonstrated the need for further decoration?" he said.

Christine Merrill's THE CHRISTMAS DUCHESS is one of three short stories in our Christmas anthology **WISH UPON A SNOWFLAKE.**

Available from Harlequin Historical November 2014, wherever books and ebooks are sold.

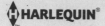
HARLEQUIN®

ℋISTORICAL

Where love is timeless

COMING IN NOVEMBER 2014

The Wrong Cowboy
by Lauri Robinson

One mail-order bride in need of rescue!

All the rigorous training in the world could not have prepared
nursemaid Marie Hall for trailing the wilds of Dakota with six
orphans. Especially when her ingenious plan—to pose as the
mail-order bride of the children's next of kin—leads Marie to
the *wrong* cowboy!

Proud and stubborn, Stafford Burleson is everything
Marie's been taught to avoid. But with her fate and that of
the children in his capable hands, Marie soon feels there's
something incredibly *right* about this rugged rancher and
his brooding charm….

Available wherever books and ebooks are sold.